AF614389

Letters To The Publisher

Nonoy Alexis

AuthorHouse™ UK Ltd.
500 Avebury Boulevard
Central Milton Keynes, MK9 2BE
www.authorhouse.co.uk
Phone: 08001974150

First published by AuthorHouse 3/3/2011

ISBN: 978-1-4567-7041-9 (Sc)

Acknowledgments

This book is specially dedicated to my parents, Rosita and Nestor, whose love poured upon me endlessly. Both of you have always inspired me to strive and be the person that I am now! Thank you for being proud of me and continuously encouraging me to do my best in all of my endeavours. I miss and love you loads forever!

To all these special people who have prayed and pushed me through the edge of fulfilling this book: Ate Rosa, Mr. Helyar, Mr. Menard, Luv and David, Juce, Rrashid,Dodoy Richard, Lenny, AJ and Ariel.

Illness is not a reason that life should come to a halt but a challenge of striving even harder and making the most at its fullest .

This book was has been accomplished when I was advised to stay at home and be away from work following a dreadful illness. I thought I could still be very productive and live meaningfully, hence, the birth of my first masterpiece.

To God Almighty, I am always grateful for the knowledge and wisdom you have graced upon me. My life has ever been so meaningful because You are there and never left me at all! All glory and honor are yours, dear Father!

This book is especially dedicated to my beloved parents,

Nanay Rosita and Tatay Nestor.

With all my love, Nonoy Alexis

Chapter One

Time at present…

Dear Mr. Fitzgerald,

I will be home very soon.

To the land where all my dreams have pondered and now fulfilled!

To the father of all my aspirations and now has become the son to create one!

After all these so many years, I have nearly arrived and came back to my home land.

As my mother once said, "bitter lemons can be turned into sweet lemonade"!

I am going home with full of pride and confidence; knowledge to impart to the youth of my generation and a hope to inspire a young person's ambition to become useful to himself, to others and society.

I will look forward with faith and turn back to the wonderful memories-good and bad, that molded me as the person that I am now.

I cannot wait to hear from you soon and will see you again, maybe for more chapters of our lives!

Please take care and be in touch.

Very sincerely,

Mr. Leandro Jawad Al Bahir

"Chicken or lamb, sir?" A young man asked in red and white suit. He was a flight steward of the Emirates Airlines.

I am on board that plane from Dubai to Sana'a, Yemen Repulic-my final destination. The country where I was born and the city where I grew most.

"Can I have lamb, please!" I replied and smiled.

I capped my pen and placed it in one of the pockets of my black, leather bag. I folded that piece of paper where I wrote the letter and slipped it inside my jacket pocket. It was hanged at the seat in front of me.

The letter is for Kevin Fitzgerald, a known English publisher and very well known to me too. Actually, I more known to him like every single detail of me.

The steward was wearing a red hat and his badge says Jamil with a Lebanese flag. He looked very handsome with a smooth face and clean shaven. He handed a tray of covered foods and offered a glass of iced water.

"Anything else, sir?

His voice was deep, in an arabic accentuated english.

"That would be all for now, thank you!"

I am seated near the window. The leg room was fantastic and the reclining chair is amazing. It's my first time to fly on a first class flight! A huge TV screen is right in front of me with lots of films to choose from.

I could smell the lamb in rosemary and apricot glaze. I paused and turned my head at the window. White clouds were passing through and nothing to view apart from that.

Seems like yesterday when I flew for the first time to London, England. But look now, years have passed and time flew quickly.

What's in store for me in Yemen? Would life treat me as how I have enjoyed it in London? How much freedom should I have the more liberty ahead of me?

I should wait and see. I would never know, it maybe be bitter but sweet at the end or sour as ever?

For now, I will sit back and relax, enjoy the flight and savor these delicious goodies in front of me. Of course, keeping an eye on that gorgeous Lebanese flight attendant is an icing on the cake. On my way home, sweet home!

"Yemen, I am coming back home!"

Chapter Two

Many years before…

The time has arrived!

It was the day when I have to leave my motherland, the country that brought me up.

The final call for all passengers of Qatar Airways has been announced.

I picked up my rucksack and proceeded to the gate where most of the other passengers were heading to. It was the only flight on that Monday morning and we were a mix of people with various skin colors.

I was very excited to get on the plane and experience being up in the air. I only brought a small luggage which I've checked in and a backpack with my jacket and a few books and printed papers about London.

The plane had eight seats in a row and I was on a window seat at the farthest end of the plane.

I was on my own and an empty seat on my left. I thought it was great to place my bag on the empty chair and enjoy reading whilst being on a flight.

I looked at the view outside and on that tiny window, I saw a vast piece of land. It was all plain and flesh with dark and blue clouds behind.

I couldn't believe it was all happening and I that time came when I had to leave my country and my parents. Things have happened very quickly and there was no turning back!

If there was a chance to see my parents and ask them about me going abroad to fulfill my hopes and dreams, I would. But it was a decision that I had to make and very significant personalities behind were so confident on that verdict. There were some other students too, but they chose to go to America.

All I prayed for was a safe journey and that London will be friendly and nice to me! That's all.

The flight had a stopover in Doha, Qatar for four hours and then flew to Heathrow, London as my final destination.

The time it reached Qatar was too quick and I never even noticed it! We flew for a couple of hours and had a very light snack on board. I had a chicken fajita and a can of coke. The flight was really calm and easy. I never had the chance to read nor looked around. There were so many worries that crossed my mind and I kept on looking and thinking about my beloved parents.

If they only knew what I was going through during that time.

The pilot has announced imminent landing and I felt being further away from my mama and *baba*. I was missing them and became more intense. They would always be delighted of what I was doing.

The plane has finally stopped and I heard numerous seatbelts unfastened and few passengers stood up and opened the compartments above us. I had four hours to wait for my final flight and I didn't have any idea what could have happened within that span of time in Doha. I picked up my bag and carried it on my back. I queued with the other passengers moving out of the plane and just followed the directions where the flight connections were. It was so exciting and it was indeed a pleasure to fly and maybe to travel.

Doha airport was quite small than I expected. There were little shops and expensive brands and really attractive. I was still in the Middle East as I have looked around and observed the people traveling and selling at the shops. I went to the gate immediately and not bothered to go around the airport. The gate was still closed and I realised, I was too early for my flight. There were some few people sitting on the metal chairs and they could have been my fellow passengers. I guessed so.

I was on the right flight to London as those people waiting were faired skin and blonde haired. They dressed differently with those men in coat and tie and women dressed with some skin exposed. I was smelling a bit of London then. Wow!

The seat was a bit uncomfortable with those hard steel but I just ignored it. I waited for almost three hours and did nothing but observed the people around me. They began to flock more and more and maybe our flight has nearly reached its departure time.

I felt a bit sleepy as I sat near the window again. There was someone next to me that during that long flight but it was fine. He seemed to be on his thirties, I wasn't sure but he was quite a smart guy on a blue shirt and fine trousers. He was very quiet and focused, reading a newspaper. He was scanning through the Financial Times. A paper I never heard of, written in english. I felt really tired and darkness has covered the space outside the clear panel. The plane has just taken off Doha and I was hearing people chatting around in little whispers. We were all settling ourselves and the flight officers were checking us all.

"I am starving!" The man beside me shouted.

He looked at me and smiled undecisively.

I looked at him and smiled back.

"Where did you have to come from?" He asked.

"I came from Yemen."

"All the way from Yemen."

"Jesus! Wow!"

"Really? That's amazing!" He exclaimed.

"What are you doing in London?"

"I am going to college in London."

"That's good. Well done you!"

"Thank you! Sir."

"Oh no. I'm not a sir."

He paused for a while and I was too shy nor sure if I maybe allowed to ask any question. He had a really nice english accent and maybe one day I could speak like him and be as fluent as he is.

The meal was and I felt hungry too as I smelled food in the air. I had chicken and steamed vegetables. I enjoyed the fruit flan and orange juice with some fizzy water and english tea at the end. I have tasted and imagined my English life during that time. We were all very quiet and that everyone was so concentrated on their food.

"Could I have another glass of red wine, please?" The man beside me asked the crew gently.

"Of course, sir!"

He finished all his food in front of him. He had beef instead of chicken but same all sorts of side dishes and dessert. The red wine must be really tasteful as he was asking for more.

"Did you enjoy your meal, young man?"

"Yes, thank you!"

"Was the wine good?"

"It's ok to be honest. I don't really expect a delicious wine in an economy class but it's fine to calm me down for the rest of the flight!"

"You're not allowed to drink yet, are you?"

"No. Never!"

"I am a muslim but I am really curious how wines are!"

"Not all of them are good, don't worry. You're not missing that much!" He grinned.

He had his second glass of wine and threw the newspaper down on his feet. He grabbed the fleece blanket and covered his legs. His eyeglasses were still on but he began to close his eyes and declined the chair. He went to sleep.

The lights were turned down but some TV screens were still on and a few were queueing in the toilet.

"Goodnight!" He whispered as his eyes were closed.

"Goodnight to you too!"

I was sure, he was referring to me and no one else.

The food wasn't too bad and I wanted to sleep too. We had like five more hours to travel and I felt a bit cold on the plane. I took the blanket as well and wrapped my whole body with it. It was nice and warm enough to cover me for the entire flight.

A turbulence woke me up and so as the gentleman next to me.

"God almighty!" He yelled.

He stood up and I saw him went straight to the toilet.

I took a small notebook in my bag. It was all plain and white. It was quite old but I haven't used it. I was thinking of making it as a planner or a diary maybe.

I was looking at the blank page and still not knowing what to write.

He came back and went back to sleep again.

The crew turned the little light above my head as he saw me with my little notebook.

"Thank you!"

"You're welcome, sir!"

I just couldn't wait to reach London and start off soon at college. I hoped to meet new friends and very interesting people along the years. Mr. Al Sadeq has arranged a transport for me from the airport to his house.

Yes, he gave me his house keys in London and asked me to shut my mouth and say nothing. I wasn't worried as he arranged everything for me in London. Of course, the IS provided a UK bank account and school papers and visa. I was so excited and really looked forward to it!

Dear Mr. Fitzgerald,

I am on my flight to London now and I just can't wait!

Everything seemed to happen so fast but I was prepared for it and ready for this amazing opportunity in London.

A journey that will take me to fulfill all my dreams and ambitions.

I always thought about my parents and just hoping that they will always be proud of what I am doing now.

May they think of me too and pray that I will always be successful as I start a new life and begin to explore the world in England.

Sir, you promised to take care of me so I really count on you a lot!

I will definitely do my very best to excel in all that I do especially in school and promise to make you proud.

You will be one of my inspirations in achieving what I want to become so please bear with me.

I will always get in touch with you so that you will know how I am doing and I hope it will always be good news.

I promise not to give you any headache and worries that will make you hate me.

All suggestions will be greatly appreciated.

I will call you as soon as I land in the English soil.

Speak to you soon.

It's me,

Leandro

"Goodluck and welcome to the UK!"

"Thank you. Nice meeting you!"

The man I met on the plane took his hand luggage from the compartment above his head and went off ahead like he knew where to go. He must have been doing this often as he looked so confident and everything was in a routine pace.

I took my bag and followed the rest of the passengers. We all ended up with other more people in line at the immigration department of the airport.

I queued to the non-UK passports sign and saw some men and women from the middle east too as their clothes showed.

I wasn't alone then.

But I dressed like a backpacker on my torned jeans and checkered thin shirt. Maybe they thought I was a student from Asia or yeah, a backpacker.

I took a clear envelope inside my bag and had them all ready. They're all my relevant papers from school, my Yemeni passport and Mr. Al Sadeq's letter, authorising me my tenancy in his house. I was a bit nervous after all! They could have denied me and sent me back to Yemen. I was warned that I will have to undergo all of that airport procedures.

I was standing at the arrival area and an old, short man came towards me.

"Sir Leandro!" He yelled.

"Yes, it's me!"

"Come with me, please."

I followed him as I continued dragging my small luggage and struggling with my backpack. He was walking fast tracking the way out of the airport. It was quite big and daunting. There were so many people rushing about and I thought I would get lost if I ever traveled all by myself.

It was a cloudy morning and really chilly just outside Heathrow Airport. The man took my luggage and headed towards a black van parked in a really busy car park.

“Thank you so much!” I tried to help him but he was fine with the luggage.

“Welcome to London!”

“Thank you!”

I went inside the car and took out a thin jacket from my bag. I felt more cold. I was like inside a fridge.

“Hmmmm….I can’t believe I am in London now!”

The car moved slowly. I was seated at the back and felt a huge breathing space just being on my own.

“How was your flight, sir?”

“It was ok, thank you! What’s your name? How did you know it was me? That I am Lenadro?”

“Ha! Mister Al Sadeq told me about you.”

“But you will be surprised because I’ve asked four people before you!” He laughed.

“Oh really?”

“That was so funny!”

“I’m Miguel by the way.”

“Mister Nasser has always been my passenger when he comes and goes.”

“I know where he lives. So don’t worry my friend.”

“Thank you, Miguel.”

“You’re welcome. Just rest then, ok?”

He had a strange accent and I can’t recognise it. He wasn’t definitely from England and by the looks of him, no!

It was quite a long journey and then we stopped in front of a low fenced house. It was a tall building in white. I can't imagine those two huge pillars in front and really unusual but interesting.

"This is your house!" Miguel exclaimed and got off the car suddenly.

"Oh, ok!"

I jumped out and went at the back to pick up my luggage. He was already standing and waiting for me there with it.

"Thank you, Miguel!"

"How much do I have to pay?"

"Oh, no. No! It's all done!"

"Call me if you need anything, ok? Take care, sir!"

"Bye!"

"Thank you so much! Bye."

I searched for the key in my bag as I was standing in the front door.

"Leandro, welcome home!"

Chapter Three

So you should know my name by now!

For the record, I am Leandro Jawad Al Bahir. I moved to the UK when I was sixteen. I was very young then but full of dreams and ambition.

I lived in Knightsbridge, London. A lot of people were really shocked on how I can afford to live there but as you may know, I was looking after Nasser's London pad as he used to call it. It is situated in Egerton Crescent, along with the other white Georgian flats. They all looked simile to other London houses. It is located in a very quiet area of Chelsea where I barely knew any of my neighbors. This three-bedroom maisonette was Italian inspired with white leather sofas and Florentian tapestries. I have a little room of my own on the second floor with an ensuite bathroom. I often stay in my bedroom with a small tele and my Apple laptop given by Mr. Al Sadeq. I seemed to have my own world inside my room with scattered books and magazines, all essential in college and some maybe not? I rarely stayed in the living area but I spent more time there when I knew he's coming so I damp dust the area and wash the Persian carpets and Dutch curtains. It's a lovely little mansion furnished with antique wooden furnitures. I imagined, the fifty inch flat tele wass the only modern stuff in the living area. The kitchen was so uniquely inspired from an old style country kitchen with a brass cooker and hanging pots and pans. The orange granite ran along the cupboard was just so magnificent.

I moved there straight away and not at the college accommodation. Nasser was very kind for as long as I look after his flat and of course take care of him too everytime he arrived. He rarely used his place anyway and stayed most of the time in hotels. I think no one knows that he owned a flat in London?

I am on my final year at the London College of Arts, Film and Theatre. It's a known university in Regent's Park where some famous artists went from all over the globe. I actually researched it before I enrolled and had to do some acting auditions on stage and proved my English proficiency. I was so pleased when I was accepted and now focusing on my major subjects in Film and Writing.

That part of London is just in between Knightsbridge and South Kensington so people call me "posh" as I reside there. I never had visitors in the flat as I am was very discreet especially my connection with Mr. Al Sadeq.

The school knows that I live with some other students in south London and my friends knew that I usually work in a club in Soho every Saturday night.

I am now nearly twenty one and feeling old after spending nearly five years in the UK. I am not that tall actually. I still have those wavy, black hair from my father. People still keep on asking where I got my bronzed skin as if I had a fake tan but actually I inherited it from my mother. I run a lot just along Thames river or even in Hyde Park as they are very close.

My Mama copied my first name from a famous actor in the Philippines who was known for his t.v. soap dramas. She was very fond of watching them when she was young. Her family could not afford a television at home but she managed to stand outside their neighbor's house at six in the evening and wait for the program. At times, their neighbor even shut the windows for her. She went to school with their daughter so Mama helped her with their schoolprojects and became good friends. The famous actor Leandro came closer to her heart so she called me by that name. The rest of my name is from my Yemeni clan. I am half Yemeni and so a practicing Muslim. I was born in Sana'a, Yemen Republic in 1988 by my parents Jawad and Suhailah. I was raised more by my mother and my father was away most of the time, working as a Chief Pilot of the Yemenia Airlines.

Mama used to read a lot of poems and bedtime stories in english and so I learned the language from home through her. If I look back now, she didn't really speak the language too well as she hasn't reached secondary education. According to her, she watched plenty of english films and read english papers. She tried to copy them and taught herself as they sounded correctly. She was funny but I'm proud to learn it from her for a start. Baba speaks more fluent english as he studied aviation in Europe so he was our main teacher. He sounded very American and he was really cool.

When I reached seven, they enrolled me to the International School(IS) of Sana'a. It was stiff at the beginning but I got along well after years of being away from my parents. Mama used to come every weekend to collect me spend the weekend at home whilst *baba* phoned me occasionally during his flights and always reminded me to be brave and bright.

I loved english, math and science. They have been my favourite ones, until we were taught to write essays and poems. I used to read my poems in front of the class and even acted as Romeo in our school play.

I remained to be just the simple student in class. I didn't receive any merit or distinction but I wasn't too bad to be honest. I also learned to play sports and be with other kids. We played tennis and baseball in the campus. There have been different students from various countries, so I have made friends with some Europeans, English and Asians too. I must not forget, I'm half southeast Asian myself.

Living and studying in London were such privileges that other youths may have not have. I was really lucky and even more lucky to have a scholarship grant from the IS. They paid all school fees and accommodation as well as a monthly allowance of one thousand pounds. Not too bad, although I still worked in a little English pub in Knighstbridge every Saturday night and come home with plenty of tips from the posh Chelsea people around the area.

I went to college, four days a week and have the rest of the week off. I had loads of time to go out and meet up with friends, work for a day and clean the whole house every Sunday. It was a routine but I can't complain!

Mr. Nasser Al Sadeq was mainly my benefactor. He financially and emotionally supported me. He knew what London life wass all about so I got a lot of advices from, being in England. Although, money was not a problem for me, I still spent less in going out but more on traveling and reading books. I love going to the movies as my Mama proved that she learned many ways of talking from them and I guessed she was right. My communication skills have improved in so many ways aside from watching films really.

Chapter Four

I studied at the Sana'a International School ran by the Saudi Aide for Academics and Culture. It is a primary and secondary school through the Saudi government to aid the rest of the Gulf. It is based just outside Sana'a- the capital of Yemen Republic. English is primarily taught by hired experts from England and America. In the early times, the bungalows comprising this little community used to be the Turkish and Jewish Quarters in the 1960's. The aide made plenty of refurbishments but still with a picturesque of the old city's tower houses with preserved light bricks and red tiled floors. The *qamariya* windows were so authentic and prevalent during the ancient times. These were intricately designed plaster and stained glasses, although the wooden enclosures have been removed. It was specifically for women, not to be seen from outside but could see people coming into the building. We were a bit isolated on a huge compound with plenty of facilities including a cottage hospital and a mini sports complex.

I thought it was a depressing concentration camp, the first time I stepped into the tall, steel gate. It appeared like an Alcatraz where none could ever escape once you're in it. The institution was fully guarded by these Indian men in green uniforms who were so stern and arrogant. No wonder, some students still managed to slip out and go clubbing at the U.S. Embassy which was quite proximal. These guards were just worth a box of cigara, few dollars or even a supply of *sadiki*- a gut burning drink with pure alcohol derived from a car battery. They must be bloody desperate for alcohol?

We were a mixed of students-quite multiracial and combined genders. I used to cry every night, missing my parents especially my mother. My teachers just dragged me outside of the classroom and left me crying inside a store room until I got very tired. I barely ate as sixty percent of the population was non-muslim so we had bacon and sausages for breakfast and roast pork for lunch or dinner. I always looked forward to the *halal* meats and vegetarian burgers but my parents' cooking was still irreplaceable.

As years passed on my formal education, I became more independent and have adopted to the sovereign society. We had a very posh accommodation with only two students in a one-bedroom flat-fully furnished. Although, we sleep on a double decked bed, it was enough for very young people to start off school.

I was seven and all I can recall was questioning each of my teachers when my parents would come and take me back home. Yet, I haven't had a clue except from my South African math teacher on her forties. She mentioned that I should start learning how to become independent. Who is independent and why should I become mister rubbish independent?

As time flew, I have adapted not so badly on that institutionalised climate and progressed spontaneously on my academics. I excelled more in foreign language especially in English and literature, particularly European and Asian. Sports became the favorite of all so I was competitive in swimming and lawn tennis. I learned how to play chess with my unforgotten flatmate Juergen. I still cherished the sleepless nights we spent together with him teaching me how those chess characters move, eat and mate each other! That was really funny but seriously, I could play the game really well. I was very eager to dare my uncle Tareq for a chess match once I got home for one weekend. He's promised to treat me to our favorite Lebanese restaurant if I ever beat him. Juergen was a special person I didn't regret to know apart from being just my flatmate or a chess mate. He was the son of the hospital director and the chief nurse. They came all the way from Munich, although, his parents were Austrian. They have travelled from different places as his parents loved working and living abroad. We shared similar stories but for him, he missed all his friends back home. I missed my parents and I envied him when they go out as a family during the evenings.

Juergen looked quite tall for his age, blonde and short-curled hair. He has gorgeous blue eyes and stood very athletic with his broad shoulders.

Quite stern I would say but must be a German thing but in fact, polite and quite a gentleman.

We were so naughty when we win against the other boys during a swimming competition. We asked all their food supplies as our reward. They were left with just orange purees and porridge as we demanded to have their custards and sausages. Sometimes, we can be very cheeky when we dumped all their clothes to the toilet sink and piss on them. Those poor boys go back to their flats naked and cold! No wonder, the cleaners got so disconcerted with the blocked sinks and flooded loo.

Juergen Schonfield was in the senior year so he must be sixteen at that time when I met him. They have just moved to Yemen for less than a year at that time but I haven't seen him having difficulty to adjust with the Arab world.

One evening, he came home following a football match and looked really exhausted.

"Lean!" He shouted as he banged the door and dropped all his stuffs on the floor.

I came out of our room just on my white boxer shorts. He actually woke me up from an afternoon nap. I should've gone home that Saturday but neither of my parents nor uncle came to pick me up. They usually come in the morning and we have lunch at the city centre but I gave up as this has happened quite a few times. Before, I used to stand outside of the flat door, dressed up with my backpack and ready for home and stood all morning and evening and not eat at all just waiting for my parents. I used to cry silently and rubbed my eyes until they get very red and sore. I thought my sight would change and view my parents coming along the cobbled path to greet me and take me home. No one arrived at the end of the day but Juergen sometimes finds me there and brings me back into the flat.

"No one loves you!"

He was only joking but it can be true, can't it? He smiled after he whispered those words and I thought, can this boy be ever serious with life? Why can't I be like him and chill out like any other boys in school?

Juergen used to bring lots of food from his family day out and really kind to share them with me. I discovered the Indian curry through him and never realised how chilly they are. Also, his mom baked delicious cakes and pastries so we shared them while he explained the ingredients and the way his mom bakes. He said, his mom always shared the stories about meeting Juergen's dad in a little coffee shop in Bregenz, Austria. They first met there and so there love story began and it was love at first sight. His mom said that the best way of cooking is to remember your happiest moments especially when you fell in love the most! No wonder those *apfelstrudel* and fruit tarts were so yummy!

I looked at Juergen on his mud soiled blue jerseys. I noticed the knee length black socks rolled down on his ankles and those black football shoes were just terrible with the spikes underneath.

"I knew it! I didn't see your parents' car so I assumed you're spending the weekend with your lovely flatmate." He was gasping for air but made an effort to finish the whole sentence with his English in a German accent.

"I'm used to it now! I don't mind playing chess with you all night as long as you let me win and not run around naked and starved like the other boys in school."

I replied with some hesitation as I know he can be cruel as I've seen what he did to those bastards in school.

"Perhaps, we can do more than that and be a bit exciting! Let me just have a shower!"

He began taking off his clothes bit by bit and walked to the bathroom. All I can see was his tight bottom and muscled back. He didn't even bother to close the bathroom door for decency's sake! But I don't mind at all. I went back to the bedroom and turned the tele on. I actually sleep at the top of the double decked bed and Juergen obviously owns the crib underneath. I was flicking through the channels and finding my luck to watch Lost. It was such a phenomenal TV series and we even have Arabic subtitles. I have always dreamed of being one of the characters on that series.

I noticed that Juergen took so long in the bathroom and maybe he soaked himself for a bath. But never mind! I have no idea what his plan was for that night, except getting pissed with the Indian *ascari.*

I fell asleep and roused when he shouted my name.

"Lean, what's this sleeping habit, huh?"

I swiftly sat up and saw him standing at the door wearing a blue towel wrapped around his hips. He was dripping all over with soapy water as I can see the tiny bubbles on the floor. He must have just risen form the bathtub I suppose? He directly sat on his bed and I have lost sight of him but could still hear him talking.

"I would love a massage! Can you do a good one?"

I sneaked with my head down first to search where he was.

"My Baba taught me like the way my mother does and he said I was really good! You bet?"

My father always loved to have his head and back massaged everytime he comes back from his long haul flights. I remembered my mom stroking her hands and fingers gently all over his back and drawing circles on his head. Baba moans and groans with his eyes closed. My father loved it hard and deep. He falls asleep right and then following my mom's soothing massage skills.

I jumped out of the deck, fell on my toes and stood right in front of Juergen. He's positioned himself flat and supinedin his bed, still with towel on. His hair was so wet and I saw his pillow damped. How graceful when water flew through the lines on his chest, defining his muscle and bone structures.

"Go on, let's see what you got!"

Juergen proned himself in bed with his head twisted and facing the door. His eyes remained closed. His broad shoulders were so defined and his spine aligned conglomerately.

I started pressing his forehead, rotating my fingers till they reach his temporal areas and grasped his blonde hair as if I tried to hold them all. My index fingers went back and concentrated on his jaw bones and feeling his neck pulses.

"Oh, what a good start! But maybe it can be a bit harder and deeper, couldn't you?

He lifted his head to make it easy for me and laid it on a damp pillow. He must have noticed it's a bit unwieldy for me, like the way I position myself.

"I don't mind you sitting on top of me. I guess that's an ideal position for a masseur, isn't it?"

I sat on his firm buttocks and continued to stroke his back and squeezed his shoulders. His skin was so smooth as I caressed and fondled them. There was silence but I ignored it. Maybe he fell asleep like my father does? Or maybe I was doing something right then without hearing any complaint?

Juergen flicked himself over and looked at me in the eyes. He looked very tired and sleepy.

"Are you ok, Lean? I thought that was fantastic!"

He smiled and his teeth sparkled. I was pleased that he liked my massage skills. I was just wondering what would I get if I disappointed him. Well, maybe he would offer me more pastries this time or let me win in chess match later?

Juergen took my hands and guided them in between his thighs. I let him as I thought he wanted his legs massaged but it meant differently. I felt uncomfortable and tried to pull back my hands but he insisted and looked at me in the eyes and nodded slowly. I felt his huge bulge and he gradually took the towel off and threw it on the floor. He grabbed me near him and we were closely facing each other. I was lying on top of him and he started kissing me on my lips. I was shocked and couldn't utter a single word. I was a bit uneasy but the warmth of his lips touching mine started to search for more.

That was the first time I ever kissed another guy at age fourteen? I was uncomfortable but I still allowed him and really liked what he did to me.

We were still kissing and he searched for my tongue with his and I offered it. He played and teased it. I can taste nothing but the sweetness that I don't know where from? Or was it a toothpaste or some pastries he just had? I cant explain! Juergen slipped his hands on my tight shorts and started pulling them down all the way through. He squeezed my buttocks and brought me closer to him tightly. I loved what he was doing to me and I cannot help myself from stopping him.

"Oh, I love that! You are so damn good!" I whispered with my eyes closed and head up in the ceiling.

He pulled and raised me as I ended up sitting on face. He was gentle, playful and very sensual. I was in ecstasy and could not think of anything else but so much joy. I knew I have to give back and be more passionate and so I was mutually chained with such a delight!

Juergen ran his tongue on my back upto my ears and whispered, "I want to be inside you, Lean."

He sounded like he was asking a huge favor. I didn't fully understand what he meant but I felt comfortable now. I was just under his spell! Somebody should pinch me if I was dreaming or rather not?

I felt him inside me and wondered how he got there? He was breaking into my walls and I can't help but cry in silence. Tears flowed gently as my eyes remained closed. It was a great joy until he came and left a part of him inside me. At the same time, he helped me to reach climax too and together, we held each other's hands with our lips converged!

"I've never felt this happy before, Juergen."

"Shhh…it's all ok!" He replied and wrapped his arms around me.

I can't believe everything's just happened beyond my control but it didn't worry me anything at all? Juergen fell asleep and I hardly could. We were still laid right next to each other on his tiny bed and I can hear him breathing deeply on that very solemn evening. I still felt him all over me, kissing and carcssing.

That night went really fast and never did I notice the breaking of dawn until I felt the heat of sunshine scorching in my forehead. I must have slept at the end! Juergen was no longer beside me and I searched for him in the room but he's nowhere to be found. I looked at the wall clock just sitting on top of our chest drawers and it was nine o'clock on a Sunday morning. I knew that he normally plays tennis with his father whilst his mom prepares breakfast for them. They also drive out to the beach and have an Indian meal at the end of the day.

Since then, I loved spending the weekend more at the school accommodation and enjoyed Juergen's company at the same time. We remained very discreet about our special connection to each other and one day, he invited me to join his family for breakfast and some tennis matches too. I had a great time and felt sorry that I did beat him and his dad. They ended up treating me for dinner at the Indian restaurant.

Chapter Five

Nasser Al Sadeq was an Operations Manager of Nazir Jubail Oil Source in Oman. The company is Gulf satellite of the British Petrol Group in England and some for Shell Global in Asia. I cannot forget the first time we came across each other and that was during an inauguration at the Hodeidah Jamil Hotel by the Red Sea. Hodeidah is one of the historic cities in Yemen, known as it sits at the heart of the Red Sea. Nasser was a very simple guy then. He was wearing a white, silk *thobe* as far as I can recall. I was invited not as a guest but to help out with the meals and aftercare in the kitchen during that assembly.

Eventually, there was a shortage of servers and so I volunteered as I long dreamt to wear those neat and white shirts with black boat tie and a pair of slim black trousers. I was full of excitement when I was asked to change into those uniforms with no idea what concierging was all about? Nevertheless, I didn't care as I wanted to see all those prestigious guests from various companies sponsoring our aide and my school. Although they wouldn't really care to recognise me-yeah, dream on Lean!

Anyhow, there I was, looking perfectly innocent on those lovely uniform pretending with all confidence. I could smell the hint of rosemary on the roast lamb that we served and cannot forget the pancakes for desert that our French chef did with generous amounts of Belgian truffle glaze and caramel. I thought they were the most delicious pancakes I have ever had! I did manage to eat a quite decent portion from a left over plate of Monsieur Frederick Cotelle- a French man representing the European Business Management Group. He must have not liked it, nor, he was sick and tired of eating pancakes all his life in France? Well, merci beaucop monsieur Frederick!

Nasser was finding his way to the bathroom and walked pass through the kitchen. He literally saw me gobbling the pancake in front of the sink with plenty of piled dishes. I looked like a mad dog but never noticed him as I was concentrated savouring the dessert. He came back and sneaked on the half-opened door.

"Those pancakes are gorgeous, aren't they?"

I was so shocked and hugely embarrassed! I wanted to reply and defend myself but my mouth was so stuffed. I felt my jaw locked, glued with chocolate and my lips sealed with caramel syrup.

Nasser just suddenly disappeared and wasn't bothered how embarrassed I was. He headed down to the toilet swiftly, maybe unable to hold himself longer and attend to his dire need of the loo. He could have reported me and got punished or dismissed? I picked up a soiled towel from the dirty cooker and wiped my whole face. I swallowed everything that's left on my mouth and took a nice deep breath. I walked down to the toilet if I may find the Arab guy. He must have headed down that way. I have to plead my guilt and apologise so he will not report me to the *modir.*

I stepped into an orange tiled floor and dark wood room. It was a huge bathroom with dark, wooden dividers.

"He must be in one of those?"

No one was in there except me and maybe him? I can smell lavender from a scented sponge or stick?

"Uhm, sir? Are you there?"

He should be there and if not, he must have reported me by now.

I heard a toilet sink flushed and the last door of the cubicle swung as he came out whilst pulling his trousers up. He seemed to ignore me and went straight to the tap, washed his hands and placed them under a noisy drier. Mr. Al Sadeq, then looked at me in a comical way and grinned.

"Don't worry, I won't report you."

Finally, he said something that allowed me to breathe in slowly and my chest loosened up slightly. I was certain, he could speak English but still with his Arab accent, maybe from the south.

"Sorry sir, it will never happen again. I deserve to be punished and maybe expelled from the international school." I replied with my head down and very apologetic voice. I could kneel down and show my sincerity as my parents would never forgiven me if they will ever know.

"Oh, so you are a student of the IS? That's why you're a clever boy, aren't you?"

I do not understand why I was clever then? Maybe, the idea of pretending to be a server to be with decent people and eat their food was clever for him?

"I am really sorry, sir!"

"Stop apologising! What you did was right! Food should never be wasted and plenty of our brothers are still starving."

His words made me more calm and I felt a bit comfortable with him. I didn't fear like I should really be, yet, he sounded so down to earth and didn't treat me like a servant who could just be jailed that time.

"I wish you good luck in your studies! Don't forget your motherland and your brothers in need. I have to go. *Ma'a salama*!"

He took something from his pocket and gave it to me. It was his business card. He quickly stepped out of the bathroom and I was left holding the card and looking at it carefully. It has his full name, office address written with his email and mobile number. I was shocked why he needed to give me his contact details?

We were driven back to Sana'a by a small van that night of the same day. There is no speed limit in Yemen and our Yemeni driver had a load of *gat* that evening. It was very late and I could barely see the road. The stars were the only light and the moon covered with dark clouds. I tried to find the views out of the window and I could picture out the dry land on a vast sinister. They must have stayed the same like how I saw them this morning and now is a time to rest and get ready for a new day tomorrow.

I took Mr. Al Sadeq's card on my pocket but I could barely see what was wriiten on it. Everyone in the van was fast asleep and I heard some snoring. I was the only one left awake and the other one was our mad driver in euphoria and ecstacy produced from chewing *gat*! I had *gat* when I was ten. My uncle Tareq gave me and let me followed him chewing it and storing the ball of *gats* in my cheeks. The juice was bitter but somehow tasteless and we looked like we had tumours in our cheeks. The *gat* leaves are known in Yemen especially for men to have pleasures in the afternoon. It makes people more awake and euphoric so it maybe illegal in other countries but medicines were derived from it as far as I know.

The van drove me last to my accommodation and I was still intrigued to know more about Mr. Al Sadeq. I didn't feel tired after that long journey to and fro but it was like wee hours of a Sunday morning. I was still wearing the odd uniform and I didn't bother to change as I really felt the moment of looking smart all throughout that day. I headed to the library and thought of looking through the databases about Mr. Nasser.

The library is open all the time with our badge as an access and you can stay there all day and night if you want. No one was there! I sat in one of the computers and searched for the names data base and searched for Mr. Nasser Al Sadeq. His details have shown and surprisingly, they were not many. He studied in Yale University with a degree in Environmental Engineering and and MSc in International Relations at the London School of Economics. Alongside, he has achieved so many awards and accomplishments that have made him become the manager of the oil company now.

"Wow, what a great achievement has he!"

He actually worked in the U.S. and Europe so he must have traveled a lot!

He was a man of inspiration and maybe I could have known him more and that includes his personal side?

The clock striked at four in the morning and my eyes have nearly dropped. I went back to the flat and just slacked myself in bed. It's

Sunday and there's nothing to do. I slept the whole day inside a very quiet flat. Alone, prepared myself for another week in school.

"Mama and baba will be very proud if I tell them about what I did that weekend."

Chapter Six

One afternoon in school, my English teacher called me to his office and that really scared me. I love my English class and tried my best to excel in speaking and writing the language. I was rubbish with the English literature but I have always made so much effort to read Shakespeare's if not write like him. I came to his little office at the back of the college building. It was full of playwright sketches on his wall. There was a tall cabinet filled with books but I can't barely identify them. They must be all English based books of various genre! There was a little office table and a black desktop computer. Damn! A PhD in English award was hanged on the wall and signed by the Oxford University in England! That wasn't a surprise? I was shocked when I saw Mr. Nasser Al Sadeq sat in front of his desk!

"Mr. Al Bahir, I want you to meet Mr. Nasser Al Sadeq. He is one of our benefactors."

"He came to interview some students who could potentially excel abroad and I chose you to be one of them!" Professor De la Mere exclaimed and brought me near to greet Mr. Al Sadeq.

I was totally astounded but deeply honored. I have never expected a meeting again with Nasser and that time was a decent one.

"My pleasure to meet you sir! Thank you for this invitation!" I yelled with a shrill and nerve wrecking voice.

Professor De la Mere left us for his English class and wished me good luck. I wasn't prepared for an interview that time and what questions were he suppose to ask? We sat in front of each other and he looked at me with a cheeky smile.

"Do you want some crepes and tea?" He asked with a smirk on his face.

I have lost the will to focus and just laughed. He hasn't forgotten the silly thing I did in Hodeidah. I couldn't believe it!

Nasser brought me to the Sheraton Hotel at the city centre in Sana'a. They have a French café and restaurant bar. Of course, they do crepes for sure but I left him to deal with it. He recommended the scallops and mushrooms with cream for mains and strawberries and chocolate for dessert. They were best paired with mint tea. Whilst waiting for our food, I waited for him to speak, so remained timid but really animated.

"So, Mr. Al Bahir, how interested are you in pursuing your studies abroad?" He asked with a deep voice.

"Very interested, sir. Please, just call me Lean like my parents do."

"I want to become a writer, study arts, culture and more become creative in literature…if possible!" I answered with great enthusiasm.

"Wow, that's a very interesting ambition! London is the best place to do those. What do you think?"

Anywhere, sir! I trust the IS and I'm sure they know where to send me especially Professor de la Mere."

Our conversation was interrupted when the food arrived. The scallops and mushrooms were exquisitely gorgeous and still looking forward for the dessert!

"Will your parents approve to the school's proposal?" He continued whilst slowly munching his food.

"Certainly, sir! They will always let me decide what I would study for college. Although, my father is a pilot, I'm sure he won't disagree. My mother always loved reading and listening to my poems and short stories!"

"Let's see what we can do then. For now, enjoy your dinner and there's nowehere to hide this time, ok?" He added.

He sounded like a naughty man. I guessed he was on his forties that time and just thought, am I allowed to ask anything about him? Maybe it was the right time?

"Do you have any questions or anything to say, Lean?" Finally, he asked!

"How about you sir? How did you manage to realise all your ambitions to achieve your position now?" I directly asked.

"Well, I studied and worked abroad as you will do, too. I focused more in school and enjoyed my life meeting people and working on different cultures."

"I spent more time in America and England when I was young, so have been moving around quite well, indeed!" He added with a serious voice.

"Your parents must be proud of you, sir. I must confess, I have read some of your resume at the library after I met you that day."

There was a moment of silence and he paused for a while and stopped eating. I felt, maybe I was too comfortable with our conversation and I should have stopped and just answered all his questions instead.

"My parents died from a car accident when I was nine. I grew up at my uncle's family and they dumped me at the IS. It was a boys' school before and ran by the *imam*."

Nasser's voice changed and sounded quite sad. I really meant to know him personally but didn't realise his past to be that miserable.

"I wish there was somebody who will be proud of me; someone who would come to school and attend my awards ceremony. But no one appeared. I always looked at the audience whenever I receive an award on stage but none of them was interested. I just received the medal and congratulate myself!" He followed with a sweet smile.

"I strived to be at the top of the class and stayed many years at the dormitory as an orphan perhaps. It has never let me down and I didn't lose hope to achieve more. I received a scholarship from the Saudi Aide to study abroad and that gave me more hope of becoming what I am right now!"

This man deserved to be where he is right now. He truly inspired me and so, I should do my best too.

"You are very lucky now, as the IS was handed over ten years ago to the Saudi Aide and the Yemeni government. You should make the most of it."

We moved on to the dessert and the strawberries and chocolates were like *gats* leaving me in ecstacy! The restaurant began to fill with some tourists, maybe French on vacation or businessmen in Yemen? Nasser did not finish his dessert and I wanted to ask him if I could take them home with me, but I thought, it was disconcerting!

He drove me back straight to my accommodation. It was nearly eight in the evening and I waved goodbye as I looked at the back of his black Land Rover leaving me in front of the housing building. He was a very interesting man and our conversations continued on our way back to my flat. He was actually married to a French lady before and got divorce after a five-year of long distance relationship. They never had a child, although Nasser tried to have one but the French woman avoided it to prevent her from scarring and bearing baby fats. She was a model and an actress. They got married in Las Vegas and met in Monaco at the casino. Nasser used to go to the south of France frequently for the European meetings. After their divorce, the French woman claimed half of Nasser's assets but that didn't really bother him as money wasn't an issue. He became so depressed so he focused more in his job and became involved with other projects. He realised, it was less painful than his parents' death nor humiliating than what his uncle did to him. I was really shocked and frozen, seated on his front car when he told me about the sexual molestation he suffered from his uncle!

I didn't know what to say nor do but he assured me that he is better now. He was young and innocent then, never had the right to fight back or ran away. Nasser spoke to his uncle's wife about it but she never listened until one day, his uncle accused him for stealing his money and Nasser was prisoned at age twelve. He had more accusations following that. Liar! A disgrace to their clan and a unanimous thief! He didn't stay long in jail because he was in a very young age. He was handed over to the boarding school for boys under close supervision of an *imam.* He thought he was better off there, away from the physical and emotional abuse his lone family did to him. But Nasser was wrong! The *imams* punished him every single night to pay all his offenses to *Allah.* They said, he will never be forgiven until he loses his tongue and hands. He was down on his knees every night, naked and cold. They beat him with nylon ropes, leaving him bruised and swollen. He never complained but thought it could bring him closer to his parents if he will ever die. He grew tougher. His colleagues bullied him as an orphan and a real disgrace to the Muslim society.

Months have passed and the institution was handed over to the Saudi Aide. The *imams* left the governance and some qualified Arab teachers became dominant. They introduced more standardised teaching and injected foreign subjects especially english, science, history and sports.

Nasser's perception of his own community has changed and he strived more to prove the wrong. He became an editor-in-chief of the school publications and he had a column with all his opinions about educating the youth from home to society. He was known to the educators and he encouraged them to attract more students and benefactors. The school acquired more accreditation and did open for female students as well. Some benefactors joined but the strongest was the Jubail Oil of Oman. From then, they hired some foreign teachers who were more qualified for specific subject matters and became popular in Yemen and the rest of the Middle East, so the International School was founded!

Nasser received some scholarship grants to study in America and chose to go to college in Yale University. He then pursued a master's degree at the London School of Economics where he obtained a distinction award for his International Cooperation and Development dissertation. I didn't know that he was finishing a PhD in Public Administration at the Paris-Sud XI University in France. What an impressive man to be inspired for!

Look at him now as the head for operations of a leading oil company in the world. I couldn't even imagine myself being involved with him discreetly and intimately. He is the man that someone should watch out for!

Chapter Seven

For many weeks, I haven't seen my parents nor heard from them. It was very strange and hasn't happened in all of my years at the boarding school. I spoke to Mr. O'hara, my head teacher. He wasn't able to get in touch with them according to him. All messages were left on a voicemail and he didn't get any reply at all. I asked permission to be driven home at the coming weekend as I was so worried. I missed my parents so much. My *baba* might be up in the air with his hectic flights but sometimes, he gets home unexpectedly in between flights or during a stop over.

I didn't sleep that Friday night with so much excitement to see my parents or even just my Mama or Uncle Tareq. A black Mercedes waited for me outside the accommodation. I recognised the driver-it was Ghaleb. I sat at the front seat of the car and I smelled the strong cigarette all over. He smoked the last bit and threw the butt out of the window with a flick of his two fingers. He acted like he's done it so many times. I wondered how often in a day he does that to the number of cigarettes he smoke in an hour or in a single day?

"How are you Leandro?" He asked and followed by an irritating cough.

"I am fine, thank you, Ghaleb! How are you?" I asked and looked at him firmly whilst him blowing the remaining smoke away.

"*Alhamdullilah*! I'll bring you home then."

Ghaleb speaks english not so badly and they were taught as the institution has plenty of foreign guests. Although he's Yemeni, he was wearing a white shirt and black trousers rather than a *tob.* He looked quite mature with a dark skin and long beard. I first met him during an induction programme where everyone in school was introduced to all who were new.

I looked outside the tinted window and gazed in the shops and houses along the way. I missed the outside world. We were quite isolated in school and lived in a little community and not bothered about with the rest of Yemen. Our house was almost an hour's drive away from the school. It is situated at the northern part of Sana'a on a residential village called *Al Hatarish.* We lived quite near the airport in view to my father's job really.

The car finally stopped in front of a black, steel gate and white cemented walls. I was home. I recognised our little bungalow from afar. We had a contemporary, Mediterranean house in all white and painted glass windows. My uncle Tareq designed it and Mama took the paintings of the windows from her collections of patterns. She loved to make sketches and interior designing, including women's clothes. I remembered she had a portfolio of all her drawings way back when she was in Malaysia.

"*Shukran,* Ghaleb!" I exclaimed as I banged the car door. He nodded and gave me a salute. I didn't think he would come back to pick me up but I was sure my parents would bring me back or maybe Uncle Tareq and Mama will.

The gate was half-opened and only Baba does that. He would always leave the gate and doors unlocked everytime he arrives. I walked through a narrow path along the white graveled floor and I could see the front garden left untouched with high weeds. I looked for the cabbages and tomatoes that my Mama used to plant at that time. It must be a season for potatoes then if I haven't seen any of the former. I was standing at our front door and thought it was closed. It was a carved, black wood bought and made in *Hajjah.* I attempted to knock but tried just in case it was unlocked. The door was left undone and I pushed it inwards.

"I will kill both of you and you both deserved to be burned in hell!"

It was *baba.* He roared on top of his lungs and his voice was coming from the bathroom in their room. I was so frightened and certain that he was referring to my mama or who else would be in he house?

I dropped my bag and ran to their room and saw him standing beside the bath tub. There was water all over the floor and the tap was still running fast with cold water I believed. There was no steam coming out. Someone just emerged out of it whilst *baba* pulled a head out. It was mama! She was dipped in the water and my father tugged her hair out as the rest of her body followed. Mama was gasping for air!

"Mama! Mamaaaa!!!" I screamed hysterically.

"Baba, please take her out of there! Please!!!"

Mama was breathing so fast but very shallow. She looked so pale and her white thin dress was dripping with freezing cold water. Her eyes were rolled up in the ceiling and I was in a panic and had no idea what's going on?

Baba ran away and looked grossly infuriated. He didn't say anything but just disappeared. Mama was on the floor and still unable to utter a single word. She seemed to be catching up with her breathing still. She started coughing and sneezing. I assisted her as she slouched herself in bed. She was shivering and I felt her skin was ice cold. I ran and took some fleece blankets from the closet and covered her from foot upto her neck.

"Mama, are you ok? What's going on? Talk to me please, mama!"

I was shaking her and knelt myself down on the bed, right next to her. I ran and stopped the flowing water from tap. The floor was slippery and the water reached the carpet of the bedroom.

"Le-an!" She finally talked.

I ran towards her and cried. Her eyes were half-opened and looked like she was falling asleep.

"What happened to baba, mama? Where is he going?"

Mama was still catching her breath and it slowed down slightly. I took a paper board from the side table and flicked it side to side to fan her. She may have needed more air but remained silent with her eyes closed and barely breathing. Her color changed as her face became a bit pinkish.

"I will get you some new clothes, mama." I ran at the closet again and looked for her clothes. They were all hanged in pairs and ready to be worn. I knew how organised she was especially with clothes. She does my closet too and everything was just very handy as she arranged them all accordingly.

I handed them to her and I removed the white cloth covering her head. Her black hair was exposed and it was dripping wet. I wrapped it with a towel and massaged her a little bit. Her eyes remained closed and she frowned a bit.

"*Shukran, shukran…habibi.*" She moaned in a low voice.

Was she thanking me for massaging her head or was it anything else? My heart was still pounding and recovering from the frightening scene not long ago.

I still do not know what happened and what has she was doing in the bath, with her whole body submerged in cold water?

"I will prepare you some tea, mama?"

She nodded and never spoke.

I left her and headed to the kitchen. I put the kettle on and prepared a pot of mint tea. We had plenty in the fridge and it's one of those things I missed from home. Mama had plenty of mints in her garden and we enjoyed it every afternoon. I sliced some lemons and took honey as well. I reckoned she might have wanted some sweets, so I grabbed some *baklava* too. I placed them all in a tray and went back to the bedroom. She was able move herself! She changed her clothes but remained flat in bed. I saw the wet clothes on the floor so I took them to the bathroom and dumped them on a hamper piled with linens. The bathtub has emptied itself now and the water has drained completely from the floor too. I came back to mama and jumped on the bed beside her. She opened her eyes halfway and stared at me with a grin. Then, closed her eyes again like she wanted to fall asleep. I covered her with another dry blanket and kissed her forehead.

"Mama, I miss you so much! I have been waiting for you every week-end."

"I have plenty of stories to tell you, mama. I have been doing well in school and meeting more friends. I miss coming home and being with you and baba."

Talking about baba, he has disappeared! Where has he gone and didn't know if he was coming back at all?

"I miss you too, *habibi* Lean." She began talking but her eyes remained shut.

"I am glad you have been enjoying school and meeting new friends. You will get used to it and enjoy being all alone…on your own." She sedately said.

"I am jealous with my other friends. Their parents come and visit them and they go out, mama. I miss you, coming every Saturday even without baba. I miss the food you prepare and the stories you read me every night." I exclaimed with excitement.

"Your baba may not comeback, *habibi.*"

"He's in a bad mood!"

"Not coming back?" I asked her.

"What bad mood? Did he miss his flights again? Or did you not cook him nice lunch, mama?"

She opened her eyes and looked at me. She smiled with her sparkling teeth exposed. Mama has very nice teeth and dark gums. She looked for my hands and squeezed them hard as she tried but felt too weak.

"You'll know why…*inshallah.*"

She brushed her fingers through my hair and caressed my cheeks. Her hand was still cold.

"I won't bother now as we have each other. So why don't we enjoy your mint tea and have some sweets. I'll prepare a very nice dinner for you later, son."

Mama sat upright on the bed and leaned back on the carved headboard. They have a huge bed with a really comfy mattress. I used to jump up and down on it and baba didn't really like it. He once told me off that beds are for sleeping and not for jumping!

We enjoyed that short afternoon tea and mama felt so much better. She hugged me all afternoon in bed and I fell asleep. I woke up and wondered where she was. I assumed she was in the kitchen preparing our dinner and I was right. I changed to my pyjamas and wore my white *thobe.* I haven't worn it for ages as we don't wear them in school. We were trained to wear shirts and pedal shorts with a coat and tie. I loved those knee-length socks and black shoes.

I went to the kitchen and mama was there. Mama was slowly moving about with her white sarong. She didn't cover her hair that time and maybe because it was still wet. She was wearing a black apron and I smelled the rosemary on a roast.

"We are having lamb chops for dinner, *habibti.* Is that ok with you?"

"Did you sleep well? I'm sure you are tired too." She was talking with her back at me.

"I feel hungry now, mama. I can smell how delicious they are!"

"Can I bring my friend one day so he will know how a wonderful cook you are, mama?" I sat in one of the dining chairs and peeled an orange found on top of our dining table. It was a bit old dry and been there for ages. No one has bothered to eat nor throw them. But it was still edible and so sweet. We had a thick glass table from Egypt. My baba bought it and was delivered for ages. It was very fragile and expensive.

"Mama, Professor De la Mere introduced me to a benefactor who will help me to study in London. I am so excited!"

"I want to study in London, mama! I want to do it…is that ok?"

I was a bit reluctant as she may not agree or had any other plans for me. Baba most likely doesn't want me to do fine arts, maybe?

"Wow, very impressive! What course is it, did they say?"

Now, that was a good remark from her. I was positive, she would permit me to do what I dearly want for college.

"Fine arts, mama. I do not know which school yet but London sounds perfect, don't you think?" I ate the orange fast and swallowed it immediately. I looked forward for her affirmative reply.

"Is that what you want to do? As long as no one forces you to do anything that you don't like, son."

"What do you do in fine arts? What will you be called, then?" She naively asked.

"What I know is, we study arts, culture, maybe writing, acting, film... dunno much, really. But I will be called an artist or just someone who studied fine arts. Maybe?" I replied with so much innocence.

"As long as you're happy doing it. Think about it and you decide."

"You don't want to be an engineer or a pilot, do you? Like your baba or uncle?"

"No way! I want to be a famous writer or director of films, mama. Maybe write a bestseller novel. That's what I want! In fact, I want to learn more english. I know, you taught me to write and speak english but I want to be better!"

"I'm glad you liked my english, son. You know it's all over the place but I do try, Lean!" She laughed.

"Dinner is ready I think! Here we are."

Seemed like nothing had happened. We had delicious lamb chops in rosemary and thyme. I ate my heart out and was so stuffed that evening. Mama prepared some mashed, sweet potatoes too with cheese and herbs. She always loved freshly squeezed lemons and makes a refreshing lemonade.

I was still wondering where my father went but mama begged me to enjoy my meal as he was extremely busy.

We stayed in our living room until late and looked at our family photos together. Mama flicked through my baby pictures and couldn't believe how I have grown so fast.

We were sat right next to each other in our brown sofa. The living area was dimmed with just a lampshade on and a crystal chandelier. There was no place like home. It was where we end the evening with lots of stories that my mama heard from her parents. Tales and myths from her Asian culture and a place where baba takes off his jacket and shoes as he arrives from his flights. He was fond of talking about the lazy people he works with and the beautiful women in his flights. Mama used to get very jealous but as the story became customary, she just got over it and so fed up about it.

"Do you want to lie down, son?" She asked.

I loved the suede sofa and how comfy it was. I laid myself down and mama placed a pillow on her lap for my head. She carried on talking about my early childhood.

"You can't barely walk and talk. I was so worried! I read so many stories in english and you were just staring at me with your innocent brown eyes. I have been saying the alphabet over and over all afternoon, you know?"

"Your baba told me not to worry and I was so in a rush. He was right!"

"Look at you now, we may not be able to chase and find you if you ever go to London. We will never be able to speak like you now and how much more if you learn proper english in England!" She sighed.

"Life is such a magic! It's a miracle, don't you think?"

"You will learn, it may challenge you and take you out of your comfort place but you'll cope and will be proud at the end!"

I heard her last few words and that was the end of the day, I remembered. I just went to sleep and again, baba hasn't reappeared or came back home that night. Maybe it wasn't the end of her conversation yet. I don't know.

Chapter Eight

Suhaila Sawarn-Nadeem means moonlight and a common Malaysian girl's name.

It's my mother's complete name!

Mama was an eldest daughter of a farmer couple in Tongod, Sabah. They lived in a little village where farming and fishing were was the bread and butter of most population. She has a younger sister and supposedly two other more siblings but died during birth due to prolonged labours of their mother. Mama said, the whole village had only one midwife who never knew about delivering babies. She only learned it constantly by mistake so the people considered her as a sent from the heavens above. She was a lady of birth, like mama used to say.

Mama and her family lived in a bamboo hut in the middle of the fields. She was born on a night with pouring rain and thunderstorms. There was nothing but old blankets and sheets to clothe and keep her warm.

Mama described their way of living like they were so poor and lived on rice and fish and most times, root crops that they boiled and ate altogether as a family. I could imagine those leaking roofs during heavy rains and the bamboo walls where you can see through, surrounding their shed.

She grew up with a very strict father who trained them to work in the ricefields at their very young age with her younger sister. Both of them went to a missionary school by the American teachers who volunteered and taught young children in rural areas of Malaysia. Mama loved being in school and enjoyed listening to short stories, fables and fairy tales.

She borrowed her teachers' english books and brought them home to read in front of her parents and younger sisters.

My grandfather noticed that mama has lost the interest to work in the farms and preferred to be in school most of the days. He wasn't happy with that so he warned her that one day, she will end up going back to the farms in order to make a living.

Mama continued to learn more in school and stayed with her teachers' dormitory so she could continue learning and studying more. She was so enthusiastic and really keen, henced, her english was extraordinary at her very young age!

One day, my grandfather came to their small classroom and found mama. He literally dragged her out of the room in front of other students and teachers. He brought her back home. My grandfather threatened to cut her tongue if she will ever go back to that foreign speaking people again!

It was very awful and humiliating! Mama cried all day and night all, alone in their little pond. She wished being out of a little cage and do the things that once made her happy. She promised herself not to grow old and die in the farm, covered with haystacks and get burned.

One stormy night, mama escaped and jumped on a truck filled with sacks of rice all the way to Kuala Lumpur. She never had any second thoughts but to get out of hell and live a life how she wanted it to be. No one has known even her mother and sister. She strolled the streets of the city and begged each and every shop for a job and a place to stay.

Mama worked in a little Chinese restaurant owned by an old Singaporean couple. She worked all day and night with lack of rest and sleep but never complained. She told herself that it wasn't anyone's fault but hers and wanted to prove something especially for her family. Her employers treated her very poorly. Mama used to sleep in the store room with boxes of noodles and canned goods. She had only one very thin sheet to cover her and made a mattress out of those cartons. The cold floor and hot room didn't change her mind of going back to her parents and live in the farm again.

Mama used to eat those leftovers from the diners' plates. Some, she kept secretly and ate them in her very dark, four-walled room. She was only allowed a single meal for the day and was never paid as she had free accommodation. She has worked bloody hard like a dog!

One day, a French-Lebanese man in his very old age had a late lunch in that restaurant. He noticed how mama worked so hard and amazing she was, serving the whole restaurant all by herself. The old man gave her his business card and told mama that he was opening a big restaurant in Kuala Lumpur. He wanted to employ her and offered a better compensation. Mama did not have any second thoughts and so she fled off from her nasty employers.

Mama had a better job in a Lebanese restaurant and proved herself being a hardworker. She became a cashier and also a head for training. Her colleagues really liked her, especially the way she dealt with customers and the manager. Her english wasn't too bad but it was better than the others who could hardly even speak the language. Mama was so proud as well as her boss.

She had then a better room to stay. A comfy bed to sleep with a little television that could hardly get a channel.

Mama was very happy then. She was sent to a special training for restaurant management and customer service. The instructors were so impressed by a very young woman who was so confident and charming. She was awesome!

They're restaurant opened another branch in Dubai so mama was told to manage it. She never said no and accepted the offer. Mama was so grateful for her boss who trusted her very much and gave her those wonderful opportunities. Her friends became so disappointed when they saw her going. She trained some other Malaysians and Filipinos to work with her in a foreign land. They were all very excited and looked forward in their new venture.

Before the day of her flight, mama went home to say goodbye to her family. She hired a *jeepney* and filled it with plenty of canned foods and clothes to surprise her parents and sister. She thought, her father will be very proud of what she has achieved and may not be able to force her to stay in the farm anymore. She has grown as a young woman who achieved some little things in life and full of dreams ahead of her. She wanted to prove some more!

Mama came down from the vehicle and ran into their old bamboo hut. She shouted and looked for her parents and sister. She found her mother sat on the bamboo floor, feeding her father with a bowl of rice pudding and a pinch of salt on a side plate. She cried! Her father looked at her and mumbled with words that she never understood. He was talking like a small child, learning how to speak. Water was dribbling from his mouth and looked very helpless! He was so thin like skin and bones. His forehead covered with prominent lines and dropped face. He used to have thick, black hair but had all fallen off and left a shiny, bald head.

Mama's mother ran towards her and grabbed her hair! She was filled with anger and resentment. She threw her out of their hut and cursed her. Mama caused her father's illness. He looked for mama everyday and ended up having a heart attack. He suffered from stroke but was never brought to hospital so he lost his speech. They became poorer and suffered from hunger and pverty. Her mother told her not to comeback again. She was to blame for her father's suffering!

Mama never saw her sister and the neighbors said she was out in the fields, working like a dog all of the days! She went to look and found her in mud, planting rice. They hardly recognised each other but connected with embraces and tears as they looked at one another's eyes. Years have passed and each one has changed so much. There were so many words to say but mama cried harder and deeper. She could have never left but stayed and not blamed for their father's condition. Her sister thanked her for coming back again and never reproached her for what she did. Mama told her that she was leaving for a work abroad but will be in touch. Mama's sister waved her goodbye in tears and thanked her for everything she brought for them. The jeepney was moving far and mama told herself that she will comeback and pick up the pieces to reunite with her family again. She was looking at her sister in the middle of the road, filled with mud on her legs. Mama was sobbing in tears. Her chest was so tight and looked ahead on the road when she barely saw her sister no more. She cursed the day that it will never happen again, the next time she'll comeback home!

I miss you mama, I do…
Your caresses and embraces, I really do.
Gentle words and those fresh breath you sigh,
In your arms, I want to die.

I love you mama, I do…
You never counted those words, but I really do.
They wrap me and I feel so secure,
'Twas so genuine and felt very pure!

I need you mama, I do…
Your comforting ways, yes, I really do.
When I am in pain and heartbroken,
You're always waiting for me, with arms wide open!

I adore you mama, I do…
Your soft and smooth skin, I really do.
Those silky, black hair and dark brown eyes,
I know it's you and no one in disguise!

I thank you mama, I do…
Your endless love, I really do.
You gave life to me and as you liked I've grown,
Dearest mama, I'm so proud to be your own!

Leandro Jawad Al Bahir

Chapter Nine

Sunday has come and time to go back to boot camp!

I always referred the school as a concentration camp. We were like inhabitants in our own little world.

I fell sleep on the sofa. Mama covered my feet with a blue silk sheet and left me to rest on that comfy furniture last night.

I slowly moved myself up and felt like I was dragging my body to rise eagerly.

I heard noises in the kitchen and the tap was running. I felt I have to piss when I heard it.

"*Sabal kier, habibi!"* She came and greeted me a very good morning.

We kissed each other, cheek to cheek. She has rinsed her mouth and it smelled fresh. Mine was horrible for sure but she didn't mind as she always does.

"Good morning, mama!"

"Did I sleep while you were telling me stories last night, mama?"

"Sorry, sorry…so much!"

I hugged her and embraced her so tight. I really missed her so much and will leave her soon that day.

"Don't worry. You must be very tired, son."

"Come, I prepared some bread and cheese. Let's eat! Rise up, *habibi."*

"Ghaleb is coming to collect you. They rang and made sure you're ready at lunchtime."

"But mama, I wanna stay here with you more. Where is baba? Where did he go, mama?"

"He must have gone back to work. I don't know, son."

"Forget what you saw yesterday. Your baba wasn't feeling well and we just had a misunderstanding. He will come back and we will come and pick you up next weekend, ok?"

She was looking around and didn't look at me straight in the eyes. She was nearly in tears but she forced not to.

"Ok, mama. It's ok"

"I understand."

"Good boy! You are our little treasure, you know that?."

"Remember, baba and I love you so much and you must do the same, no matter what happens. And you must honor what your parents say, ok? One day you will understand and when you become one, you will realise the value of this."

"Yes, mama." I nodded and felt I was missing her more.

Ghaleb came so early and we just finished our morning tea. I didn't have much to pack. Mama walked with me outside and reassured me again of our next meeting soon. I wrapped my arms around her waist in front of our door and kept on smelling her. Her fresh clothes and warm breath bound us together and I could have stayed beside her forever.

Ghaleb came early and was in a rush as he was picking somebody at the airport that day. He was all set and ready but I was still stuck at my mama's.

"You'll be good in school, ok?"

"Be a good boy and listen to your teachers. Be friendly to your colleagues, Lean."

"Go on, son…The future awaits for you."

"I love you. We love you, *habibti!"* She cried and embraced me. She never showed her face but held my head firmly.

"Mama, please let me stay!" I felt very emotional too and wondered what was going on?

Ghaleb horned and we were both startled.

"Now, go! Ghaleb is getting grumpy."

She took me to the car and I sat at the back seat. She closed the door and waved her right hand. Mama placed her hand on the window screen and I did the same too but the glass separated us and we didn't feel each other.

"See you on Saturday, mama!" I gazed at her and knelt on the seat as the car moved slowly away from where she was standing.

Suddenly, baba's car arrived and I saw him in a rush. We were quite a distance and not very far.

"It's my baba! Baba!!!"

"Ghaleb, stop and go back! Hurry!!!"

"I want to hug my baba, Ghaleb!" I screamed and shook his shoulders.

"I am running late and a *modir's* son is waiting for a long time now!"

"Sit down!" He continued to face the road in front and wasn't bothered about me.

"Baba!!!" I cried and saw my father from afar and getting smaller as we moved away fast.

I saw him coming out of his car and grabbed my mama. He dragged her inside the house. Was he holding a gun? I wasn't sure but there was something on his right hand and I could barely see it anymore. They disappeared and went inside the house. Ghaleb has driven quite far now. How did I miss that? I missed my father?

I was still in tears but I slouched myself on the seat and put the seatbelt on. He drove faster.

"Bang!" A loud noise heard coming from like where our house was. It was like an explosion!

"Baba?" My heart was pounding and my chest expanded widely.

"Mama?"

"Ghaleb, what was that?" I asked the driver and he just shook his head.

I didn't notice that we were already at the airport until a young, blond guy swiftly came and sat beside me.

"Hello!"

I didn't respond and was still in shock. My thoughts were still with my parents and so unsure about what happened?

I remained in tears and didn't speak at all. Ghaleb drove us back to school and I remained speechless. I wasn't interested to talk to anyone and the two men conversed with each other at the end. I was so disturbed but was also very confused. Both men didn't even ask how I was doing as they saw me in tears. But I'd rather would let them leave me alone and not speak to me at all.

I was walking near the flat and felt not so at my senses. I opened the door and sat on the small sofabed. It wasn't as comfy as ours at home. The flat was so quiet and the atmosphere was so empty. Juergen must still be out with his parents.

I still felt so stuffed of the late breakfast with my mama. I remembered I brought some lamb chops for dinner but I will share it with Juergen. He loves roast lamb and I enjoyed sharing meals with him and anything in him!

As I continued being alone and silent, I felt my heart pounding louder and pushing against my chest even harder. Something wrong must have happened?

Chapter Ten

It was a sunny, Sunday afternoon. My head seemed heavy and heavier. I walked into the bedroom and saw some empty spaces. Juergen's stuffs were missing. They were not there anymore! His soiled clothes that I used to see all over the floor disappeared. His football, tennis racket… his books and his tangy linens! They have all gone!

"Juergen?" I have spoken a single word at last!

There was no answer. I ran outside the bedroom and went to the bathroom. His shower gel, aftershave, stinky towel…none of them was there!

"Juergen, where are you? You must be kidding me!"

"This is not a good joke!" I shouted and walked outside the house.

I ran at his parents flat but I couldn't get in. It was locked. I knocked and no one answered.

"Juergen! Juergen!"

"Open the door. Please!" I was crying out loud and nearly broke the door.

"They have left!"

"They went back to Germany, early this morning!"

A woman came out of the door in front of their apartment. She was quite young and I don't recognise her.

"I am Carolina, a nurse in the hospital." She exclaimed.

"Mr. and Mrs. Schonfield flew back home at an early dawn today. Who are you?"

"I am Lean, their son's flatmate." I replied in a very said voice.

I stood at their front door and looked down on the floor. The German flag doormat was still there. Was she really serious?

"Thank you, ma'am. Thank you."

"I didn't know. Do you mind if I take this doormat with me?"

"Entirely upto you!" She spoke in a Spanish accent.

"Ok, bye!"

She went back iniside her flat and closed the door slowly and locked it. She didn't even tell me how did it happen. Or maybe she doesn't know?

It wasn't a great day at all. I was so baffled and really mixed up. I have to wait for Monday to telephone home and find out about my parents. I missed my parents and didn't speak to my baba. I wished I was wrong with my gut feelings.

I was all alone in the flat that evening and didn't feel like eating nor do anything. I opened the closet and it was half empty. Juergen's clothes have all vanished. He was gone and never did I have a single clue, why?

I laid myself on his bed. Just a mattress left and nothing else. I could never even smell anything like him. Nothing!

"I cant believe you just left like that, Juergen."

"I thought you only do that to others and not to me. They are all right! You've all treated us so badly! It's not fair, is it?"

"You hurt me more though. Worst!"

My eyes became so sore and I couldn't help but cried. I was looking up at the rear side of my mattress. So he used to look up on me then? My back...my front...my bottom. I wondered why! I was imagining him laid right underneath me, behind me.

"Where are you, Juergen? I need somebody to talk to, to hold me and whisper to my ears that everything is fine. Where are you?"

I closed my eyes and reminisced the days when we're together during those sleepless nights, those weekends when we realised just the two of us and no one else. They were good old memories now. Juergen has left and I didn't have a single clue. That was very cruel of him…hurting me so badly.

I went back to my own bed on the upper deck and found a white envelope on my pillow. My name was handwritten in a black ink outside. It was Juergen's penmanship. I immediately opened it and torned the envelope, very curious what was inside of it. It was a letter. He wrote me a letter in the end!

Dear Lean,

I will be miles and miles away maybe now but here's what I have to say for all the wonderful times I have spent with you and only you…

I will miss you and will always think about you wherever I am right now and all through the years ahead.

I enjoyed my short stay in Yemen with my parents and how fortunate I am to have known you and have you as a special part of me.

My parents have decided to go home drastically and I have to leave as well.

I just wished that I could have spent more time with you if I only knew then, I would have never wasted each and every second of it.

You made me happy, Lean! You are the person that someone should know and treasure the most!

I wish our paths will come across someday and I am really looking forward to that already!

Best wishes mein schatzly!

Lots of love,

Juergen

It was a goodbye letter from Juergen. Why was I hurting so bad? I wanted him so much too and I truly loved him. He was one of a kind! But he's gone and he has left me. Why didn't he stay and let go of his parents. It's just rubbish him writing that letter. There wasn't even a contact address nor anything to reach him and find out why did he have to leave me that way? I couldn't wait too for the special day when our paths come across again. I do really look forward to that as well!

Chapter Eleven

"I'll see you shortly Kevin."

"Bye!"

I slipped the phone on my left jean pocket. I was heading to Tunbridge Wells in West Sussex. I think it's the best place to live in the south of England. Kevin Fitzgerald is an independent publisher and lives with his wife, Sandra. They have been married for twenty years now but didn't have a child as Sandra has blocked fallopian tubes and eventually lead to cervical cancer which was diagnosed five years ago. Her uterus was removed straight away and luckily, the cancer didn't spread anywhere else. I can say, they still have become a happy couple even just the two of them. They both have traveled around the globe and very successful in their professions. Sandra retired as a foreign language teacher when she suffered from cancer but she continued to be her husband's assistant in his other endeavours.

Kevin used to work at the Devonshire Publishing in London until he became the Lead for International Publishing. He has been tasked to encourage foreign authors or buy stories and publish them under their name. He has brought home so much profit and corporate stability in the company until he realised he was counterfeiting other people's work and stealing their identities. He resigned but continued as an independent publisher after being eloquent in his craft. Because of his international relations, he became the chairman of Shell Foundation and volunteered to some countries in Asia and Africa as well as the Gulf. He promoted and wrote a lot about Shell Charities and publicised projects supported by the oil company which that attracted them more donors from other institutions.

Kevin awarded me at school in Sana'a when I won the poem writing contest in my junior years. Everyone was so shocked that time especially the school paper editors as they were expected to top the competition. I have even forgotten the whole composition but all I can recall was the lesson learned from the poem and it was about the true virtue of discipline down to everyone's belief. Others were very touched on how a very young person can write such principle but for me it was one of the happiest moments in my life even without my parents. Nasser was there anyway. Those men really inspired me and took off their hats on me. On that occasion, Kevin came to me and made a proposition that I thought has really changed my journey of life completely. He was in the middle of a project and part of which was to feature an academe that the institution has produced and would like to develop. He wanted to write a journal of me, my life and my involvement with the institution. I didn't have any second thoughts and wanted to start straight away and so does he. We had all the conversations and other arrangements as he was traveling back to England and so forth.

He was on his early forties. Tall, blonde and quite fit. I still had no idea what a typical Englishman looked like during that time but he was very polite and was such a softspoken gentleman. I entrusted him the story of my life and he encouraged me to come and study in England if I was interested in arts, literature or language. The aide supported everyone of us to our desired in university. The agreement was to study abroad and comeback to our homeland and serve our community in return for all the costs they spent which was really fair.

Kevin and I have been in touched all throughout and I never imagined being asked by him with so many questions-I mean personal questions. He promised he wouldn't publish everything that I told him. I thought he was gay but I saw his gold wedding band and reconfirmed it from him- he is a happily married man and definitely straight! I wasn't really attracted to him to be honest but with our constant communication, we built a wonderful rapport and true friendship. He must be doing something right or maybe he only meant business?

The southwest train has reached Tunbridge Wells and I just felt a bit sluggish from a night out in Soho the night before. It was the beginning of July and I can feel the warmth of summer. The countryside was way opposite from the ecstatic London and I can say that I'm in the right place as I may never ever live apart from London or else I'll end up hanging myself of depression of being away from everything!"

I walked out of the station and saw Keven's car. He drove a blue BMW N-series unless he's changed it? But I can see him gazed at the window with his brown sunglasses!

"Hello naughty boy!" He shouted and appeared to be expecting a kiss from me.

"Hello mister publisher!" I went straight to kiss both of his cheeks and I could smell a lovely summer aftershave. I felt his sunglasses pressing my face. He looked so summery in his brown shirt and white jeans. I noticed he was wearing just leather slippers but anyhow, it's summer for an Englishman. I guessed?

"How's school and the London life, darling?" He asked whilst driving on our way to their house.

"Here we go again!" I replied with a sigh but he must be doing his job again and I should be used to the usual interrogation of Mr. Fitzgerald.

"School is getting more laborious but actually a lot more interesting as I come to the final end! So many projects and not really looking forward to the dissertation but everything is well, thank God!"

"Excellent! Sandra has prepared a special lunch and we will be out in the garden today. Is that ok with you?"

"That's absolutely fine! You know I'm easy, Kevin?"

"I will actually e-mail you some more stuffs for your stories. Or rather transfer them today. I brought the USB anyway. But thank you for all your help. I'm always grateful for all your support, you know that mister, don't you?" I looked at him quite seriously but his eyes were on the road constantly.

Apart from the money that I got from my scholarship, Kevin provided me some financial support too. He facilitated my university proposal in creative writing, film and arts, that's why I came to this point of my career.

This was never even known to his wife and I was sure Sandra would disapprove if she would have ever known. She has never been pleased with me and maybe thought I will steal her husband from her. I can say she is prejudiced and racist especially when I heard her moaning about some immigrants coming to England and obtaining support from then government. Or, just mentioning my American accent when we first met. But not anymore! I could speak English, the English way now after all these years spent in England.

We arrived at their house. They have a wide front garage with pebbled floors and their house was an amazing modern English country house with four bedrooms and a huge garden at the back. I loved their conservatory which is made of glass and oak wood. Plenty of books from any genre, so you can spend all your life reading them under the sun on a glass roof or maybe beneath the stars or a full moon at night?

I saw Sandra in their old style country kitchen. She was wearing a floral apron but underneath she was clothed with a pink, thin dress and leather sandals. She still looked younger than her age as she was nearly fifty. She hasn't really appreciated it everytime I tell her that. But I am really sincere, honestly!

"Hey Sandra!" I walked near her and kissed her on both cheeks and forced to hug her.

"You look very pretty!" I added and gave her a green bag from Harrods. I bought her some fruit teas that she really liked but of course I didn't expect her to show some gratitude, as usual?

"Lunch is ready so we can all head to the garden, guys!" She exclaimed as she laid the bag on her side table and carried a bowl of green salad.

"Did you want me to help you with anything at all?" I asked as I was following her heading to the garden.

"No, everything's all set as I've said!" She replied with her brows crossed.

I am used to those expressions and to be honest, I wouldn't really give in as I have a great respect for them both. I grew up with so much principles and virtues from my parents and will ever be proud of them. I still admire Sandra for her strength when she was battling cancer and how she survived it without giving up. I looked up on the two of them for their support for each other and the love they shared even without a child nor their behavioural differences.

Kevin was running towards us as we were all seated and just waiting for him. He's wearing his thick glasses and changed to a pink shirt that coordinated his wife's dress. You can say he reads so much with those frameless Cartier glasses but it fits him and looked like a genius.

We were sat on these dark wooden chairs and I can smell the rosemary and thyme from the roast beef. The twist of lemon and vinegar from the salad's mist was irresistible.

"This is such a joy having a Sunday roast with you guys. Thank you for having me here!" I broke the silence and began pouring the French red wine into their glasses.

"Let's all cheers for that!" Kevin exclaimed and we all held up our glasses.

The wine was delicious and I felt it chilling my throat. The sweet aroma of oakwood ran into my nostrils but it was heaven as I closed my eyes and savour the goodness of the vine. Muslims should have no alcohol but the English culture has influenced me a lot especially turning my beliefs from what my forefathers have taught me only when it comes to treating women and taking alcohol. What a a piece of rubbish?

"When are you coming back to Yemen Leandro?" Sandra asked as she served us all with the salad. Kevin commenced slicing the meat very gently and stared at me.

"I will be finishing soon and hope I will receive some merits. I am not sure of going home as I have no one to go home to. I still want to find out what happened to my parents. I never received any replies from them by all means?"

"I cannot see anymore reason to go home as far as I can see?" I answered with a serious voice and Kevin was looking at his wife with both eyes opened wide.

"Well, I just thought the idea of you being in this country is merely education and then you go back and pay tribute to your country? I'm sure the Saudi government will hunt and bring you back, won't they, Kevin?" She looked at her husband with skepticism.

I just thought, here we go again! She just doesn't want me in her country to be honest and we all know that. I don't bloody depend on her government after all and besides I was living a life on my own independently. What was she on about again? I didn't give her a damn shit anyway. She's my benefactor's wife! I was thinking that they were still in connection with my former institution so they can bend everything and turn my worlds apart. I should be very careful and ignore Sandra's prejudices.

"This meat is lovely!" Kevin changed the pace of the conversation. He gulped more wine and stood up hastily.

"I am off for desert so I'm gonna go and grab it if you'll excuse me, guys!" Kevin ran back to the kitchen through those cobbled stone path.

The garden was filled of orange and lavender tulips. A short orange tree gave us a bit of a shade and through the edges, various sized lime stones corresponded to the green fine grasses growing in between the rocks.

"I am hoping this will come to an end soon as my husband is only featuring you on a three-paged magazine and not a book Leandro?" Sandra spoke in a soft voice making sure no one would hear except just the two of us.

I pretended that I didn't hear anything and felt the gentle breeze of summer. The wind was crisp and fresh and my peripheral vision viewed the swaying of the orange leaves gracefully. Some brown leaves fell into the green grounds and the atmosphere was so amazing. It reminded me of being in the English countryside. Wherelse?

I swallowed my food and looked at Sandra. She was still staring at me blankly, waiting for my reply. I sipped a bit of the red wine and felt the thin glass on my lips. I cannot believe this lady still looking at me like I don't have the right to exist. Or someone who would rob her husband and will ever disappeear?

"I am hoping too, Sandra! It will be a great story and an example for the youth and those in search for love and happiness!" I replied with no hesitation.

The fact that I am gay and I came from a muslim family shouldn't really be an issue to her and her English heritage. Also, Sandra initially had doubts that Kevin and I could have developed into some sort of a special relationship but for the record, he was just like a father to me and I fully respect him for everything that he did for me. He has that great confidence in himself too as being a man I believe. I was just wondering what Sandra thought of the other subjects that Kevin wrote about. He has written so many things about people from different walks of life and who am I to be envied about?

Kevin was approaching us holding a huge plate of fudge brownies and thank God for that! Mrs. Fitzgerald could just stop picking on my blessed personality!

I smelled the warm chocolate as Kevin came nearer. I can say that those brownies were bought and not made from home. Must be from M&S or Paul's? Let's have a try and then find out!

Kevin served those to each of us and so our little conversation has halted and pretended smiling at each other with the enjoyment of a great company on that Sunday afternoon.

"Lean, why don't you stay for the night and we can go out to the pub for dinner?" Kevin asked with such an enthusiasm.

"Oh no, I'll be very early for school tomorrow and in fact, I have to finish some film reviews and literature. Definitely some other time, Kevs?"

"Mind you, I have to leave early as to avoid the rail services back to London. I am really having a nice time with you guys as always!" I replied with a smirk, finishing off the fudge quickly and felt them staining my teeth.

"That's a very sensible thing to do, Lean! You're so responsible and organised. I think that's a good investment for your future when you become more professional on your career!" Sandra verbalised in a completely and utterly change of attitude.

She was a mother fucking bitch! Excuse my language but that was Mrs. Fitzgerald. I have known her so many years. She was in fact a very interesting person and her husband should write a story about her.

I didn't stay too long that day and thought it was like a "hit and run" after having just a Sunday roast with an English family and that was it! They should be used to me or we actually should all be used to one another.

Kevin drove me back to the train station even when I insisted that I can just take a cab. I knew Sandra so much through Kevin as well and undeniably, he was aware that Sandra doesn't really like me being a part of their family at all.

"Lean, you are so matured now to understand my wife, right?" Kevin asked as he tried to look at me but continued to concentrate on his driving.

"Oh, of course! I'm ok honestly, Kevs!" I replied with a grin.

"Before, I thought I am only doing this because we had this agreement. I became to know both of you and are really special to me. So I fully understand Sandra, don't worry."

We've reached the station and it was a bit quiet knowing it's Sunday with all those journey interruptions. Kevin gave me a hug and I kissed him on his forehead. He was like a father to me and looked after me so well. I felt that he was not only after my lifestory but has became like a guardian to me. Even so, he never got too personal and interrogative to every decision I made in my life.

The train was very slow and stopped at various towns which was usual for a rail service. I was glad that I didn't have to use the coaches and transferred from one train to another. The English countryside was amazing with all the vegetables on a huge piece of land. The animals were all out in the fields bathing under the warm radiance of summer and people were on their summer clothes having a nice Sunday off!

Dear Kevin,

I had a wonderful lunch with you and Sandra!

May thank you for now but much more to come as I look forward for more Sunday roasts to come.

Don't worry, I do understand Sandra and I feel for her. She has been through a lot in her life and so as you do, too.

I always try to be a person with manners and respect for others, especially for women.

I always wish, Sandra can be a mother to me like the way you treat me as your son.

I really miss my parents and our Sunday lunches too.

I'm near London now and just thinking about what's in store for me in the week ahead.

How I want to comeback for another Sunday with you guys, again… soon.

Take it easy, sir.

Sincerely,

Lean

Chapter Twelve

"Ciao darling! I whispered on my mobile phone seductively as Mr. Sadeq laid naked on a silky beige and comfy kingsize bed in a royal suite at the Mandarin Oriental Hotel in Knightsbridge, London.

"I should see you soon". I proned myself on the bed with both toes up. He came out of the bathroom on a fluffy white bathrobe, still, with dripping long black hair. He's a Arab man on his fifties with dark green eyes and still looked fit without a bell.

"You get ready and we go for lunch!" He yelled in a Saudian accent. He suddenly dropped his robe off and exposed himself naked in front of me.

"Or you want to have me more inside you, *habibi*?"

Habibi means darling in arabic.

"I would love to, Nasser!" I replied then suddenly stood up and hugged him snugly. I wrapped my hands on his behind.

"You promised to bring me to the Armani shop, didn't you? So why don't we move our arses and hit Sloane Street!" It is thirty past one in the afternoon in London with an odd sixteen degrees temperature at the end of spring. At that time, Knightsbridge was immensely buzzing with all the young tourists from Europe in par with their very strong currency against the sterling. Sloane street is so eccentric compared to fifth avenue in New York maybe because there isn't any sale ongoing. Everyone loves Sloane Street, London; not knowing how highly marked the prices can be!

This is my life now, being a Londoner! I can't imagine myself going back to my homeland, Sana'a. This is what I love after being confined to Mr. Nasser Al Sadeq. I was able to sort myself out because of him.

I remained sat at the edge of the bed on that hotel room and thought, what my life would be, if I ever go back to an appalling experience in my past? Until now, they have been haunting me. I felt dreadful as they take me back but I resist.

Nasser was all dressed in a blue coat and tie. He was flying back to Oman that night and I will be alone again and would have no idea of his next return. We had a light lunch at the local Lebanese restaurant in Knightsbridge that afternoon. Afterwhich, we parted ways and left me four hundred sixty pounds gathered from his pockets. He wouldn't need them anymore as he was heading back to the Middle East.

As I was walking back home, I still kept on asking myself why I need to write myself down? After all, some other students could have more interesting experiences in life than I have. As I am indebted to the publisher, I'll carry on then!

Dear Publisher,

Thank you for giving me the opportunity to share a little journey of my life.

To be honest, I really do not know how to start or where should I begin?

Until now, I still feel that I had some wonderful years of joyride and some where challenging voyages that I have unbelievably gone through.

Apologies for the delay and a never-ending gratitude for all the advances or should I say…royalties. Shukran or I'd be English this time…Cheers matey!

Kindly be honest and tell me what you feel about it. You may never have to publish it but in that case, 'tis will be 'tween you and me, sir?

I am imagining you and your thick glasses whilst flicking through the following pages.

Best wishes, Kevin!!!

Goodluck!

Yours truly,

The Writer

P.S.

I'd like to have the first published copy with an autograph, please. Merci x

Chapter Thirteen

It's 3:00 a.m. on a chilly Monday morning. I woke up in a middle of a very deep sleep. I was gasping for air and became really tachypnoeic!

"Oh for fuck sake!" I was shaking my head with all the hot sweats dripping from my forehead. I sat at the edge of the bed, half naked and started to shrug my shoulders. Tears flew slowly from my tired brown eyes. I realised it wasn't just a nightmare but a humiliating experience haunted me again! At twelve, I was sexually abused by my father. A flashback crossed my mind as he was leaning himself behind me inside me from behind in our dining room at the old house in Sana'a. Baba threatened me with one of his *jambiya* collections and thought I had has the most tight hole he has ever ripped and bled. A voice whispered in my ears, " You are like your mother, you fucking whores!" He yelled as he released and came inside me. Jawad was my father and originally from Yemen. He worked as a co-pilot at the Yemenia airline where he met my mother, Suhailah. She was a passenger in one of his flights from Doha to Sana'a. Mama was very innocent at that time when she fled from Kuala Lumpur taking herself to a destination she never have heard at all. She was eighteen and during that time, she had enough of poverty and child labour from her family and country. Suhailah is a genuine Sabah-Malaysian by race. Only five foot and two inches in height, she portrayed a dark, petit and very innocent woman from the southeast Asia. She was offered a job from a Lebanese-French businessman from Tripoli. At that moment in her life, she felt it was the only opportunity to survive the realm of her heritage.

Mama escaped from her employer during a flight stopover in Dubai where she met baba in a very admiring pilot uniform along the vivacious Duty Free shops at the airport. The Yemeni pilot noticed her beauty and innocence in her long, plain *abaya* as she effortlessly portrayed a bona fide muslim woman.

"Baba, I wish you are in peace and full of contentment, *inshallah*! You have given so much of your great life in exchange of me and mama. I still owe you my life and what you have done for me was not enough to repay you. Thank you, *shukran* my dear father!" My eyes were flooding with tears as they turned red. The thin, red stripy sheet fell on the floor as I stood up and slowly walked across the room. I was only wearing a black and white underwear, quite tight as my round bottom can be shapely noticed with a cute bulge in front. I walked out of the room and headed to the kitchen, looked for milk in the fridge but there was none. I grabbed the half-filled bottle of Evian and drank it straight away. I felt very dry and thirsty and noticed it was freezing cold as it stayed in the fridge for a long while. It irritated my throat and I coughed like I was choking! I stopped drinking and still continued to stand in front of the fridge and all I can see was an empty case with a bright light and the rest of the living room appeared very dark. That side of the world was still asleep! The surreal calmness was deafening to my ears. I wanted to scream so everyone will rise and agonise with me. But that was part of a bitter past and I swear not to travel that way again!

I still hoped my parents are well upto then. Five years and I haven't heard from them and that wasn't really how they raised me. I grew up with full of love and affection from my them, especially with my mother. I saw how she sacrificed and served my father too.

"But how are they now and where the hell can I ask about them?"

I went back to my room but I guessed it's no good to go back to bed at six in the morning. I stepped into the cold blue tiles of the bathroom and turned on the shower. It was freezing cold and that's what I wanted! I wanted to be woken up from that dark past. The shower gel smothered all over me but what my father did still crossed my mind. I hated him when he did that to me!

"I fucking hate him and can't forgive him for that. I felt so helpless on those moments when he was all over me and in control of me."

I stepped out of the shower still naked and can't find the towel.

"It must be on the bed!"

I walked towards the closet and found a new blue towel and started drying myself off. I opened the closet again and searched for some clothes that I haven't worn along time ago. That was a new day and thank *Allah* for that. Going to school was always exciting to learn new subjects and knowingly, I was seeing Claudio in our photography class. I had to look my best! Although, he always told me that I was the most gorgeous Asian guy he has ever met. Not sure if that was a compliment or a complex? It was supposed to be warm day, so I wore a thin, light blue shirt with rolled sleeves. I paired it with a torn D&G jeans that Nasser gave me many years ago. Claudio thought I was Mohammed Al Fayed's grandson as he looked at me as very posh and classy. But he didn't realise I came from nowhere and just a very simple and ambitious guy. I slipped into my white Converse shoes as they were so comfy and cool especially when I used to walk across Regent's Park.

"I think it will be a very promising day today!"

That's the good thing of living on your own. You have no companion but yourself, yet, you can always say anything about you without other people's comments or suggestions.

I gathered all my stuffs and nothing much to bring except my camera and my laptop. I grabbed my camera from its bag and it looked so lovely. I bought this Canon 50D a year ago as a birthday present to myself. I got it from a loan but paid for it now after saving money from all my benefactors. I just attached a lovely 50mm lens and that will do me good. Thanks to all of them!

I walked out of the house and blimey, I looked like a tourist with my fancy camera on top of my chest. The weather wasn't too bad and a bit chilly but will be warm for the rest of the day. I don't usually eat breakfast when I go to school but loved a huge cappuccino as I got off from the bus. Whilst waiting for the bus, I put on my white earphones from my phone and turned on the music channel on the applications. I loved Gay FM and the music they played could just start my day right.

Whilst sitting on bus 74 to Baker Street, I was still disturbed on how to search for my parents and maybe get revenge for my father. This will all have to stop and he has to pay the price for hurting my mother. I was still wondering what happened after that loud explosion as I turned my back away from home? Was it my mother? If she was still alive, then, she would search for me and ask me to come home. And if my father was still alive, I deserved to be alone like this and he would he really care at all? If both of them have gone, then, this is the reason why I am being looked after by all these men surrounding me. I still should feel very fortunate instead of being dependent to the British government and poor tax payers!

I will persuade Mr. Al Sadeq more and beg him that I want to be reunited with my parents again. Or maybe go back to Yemen after school and surprise them all?

My uncle Tareq should be the best person to be asked and acquire information from. Where is he and how can I ever be in touch with him unless I ask Mr. Nasser?

Chapter Fourteen

My father was the eldest son of a clan chief in Ummul Island of Aden. Actually, he was a child from the second wife, but still very fortunate and influential. Uncle Tareq was his only younger sibling and both of them were brought up in Sana'a. They both went to the same school at Sana'a Polytechnique University.

When he was young, he spent most of his childhood with his mother andbrother in Sana'a. His father rarely saw them as he was based in Aden with his first wife and other children. Baba and my uncle were never deprived of all the good things in life. They lived in a big house in Sana'a and both of them went to some private schools for boys and exclusive French tutors. Baba and uncle Tareq enjoyed each others company with a little age gap. They didn't need other peers to hang out with but they both traveled with their mother to Europe and America and discovered the world. I remembered them saying that they begged to live in Orlando, Florida to spend their days in Disneyland. They both spent most of their birthdays in Disneyland-either Paris or Orlando. They both had a fantastic time during their childhood.

They only got separated during their college days as each wanted different vocations. They still went home to Sana'a during school holidays and spent time for their mother. My grandmother, although I haven't met and knew her personally was very loving and caring. Baba said, she never questioned her children about anything they wanted. She just approved of things and gave her children all their needs without a doubt. Baba and uncle were so spoilt then but they both remained disciplined and wise as my grandfather was such a utilitarian but very strict and humble inspite of his power and wealth.

Baba finished a degree in aeronautics and had accreditation for international compliance in École Nationale Supérieure de Mécanique et d'Aérotechnique in France. He really loved his profession so much and very passionate about it.

He started as an apprentice at the Yemenia Airways and excelled as a top trainee so his first assignment was local flights from Sana'a to Aden and vice versa.

He spoke English, French and Arabic very fluently so his level of communication to his colleagues and business partners were superior. Baba received plenty of employee awards and recommendations from his supervisors.

Baba attended some various international aeronautics conventions and conferences. He represented the airline and the company and has been rewarded for his achievements. He was indeed a great asset to the Yemenia Air.

To be honest, I have only gathered all these information about him from mama and uncle Tareq. Baba doesn't talk much about his childhood. All I knew is that he was a man of honour and deserved so much respect as my father and my provider. I never questioned him about anything that I consider non-sensible nor something that would make him doubt his integrity. I don't think he will ever like that?

Baba, thank you very much!
My father, provider of all as such!
You're the reason for my being…
My strength and pillar, I love leaning.

Baba, I want you really much!
In times of troubles, I long for your touch.
Your deeds left me wounded and brokenhearted,,,
Don't need them now as you've departed.

Baba, I despise you so much!
You left me weeping enclosed in a hutch.
You put me down and never helped me back…
Nothing I can do but get up and pack!

Baba, I truly love you much!
Whatever and wherever we'll both clutch.
I will see you sometime, somewhere…
You and I will be forever there!

Leandro Jawad Al Bahir

Chapter Fifteen

It was an early summer in June. London has never been like that for so many years. The English weather has became popular then and not the old four weathers in a day. It was eighteen degrees in central London but we flew to Perugia for our photography project. We were brought to Perugia in the region of Umbria, Italy. The weather was warmer than in London and it was my first time in Italy after a long discussion for a visa application at the Italian embassy. Those Italians thought I was a terrorist as usual with my Yemeni passport. I can't believe some people are still discriminating and racist?

Thank God for my university's full support. Claudio had the same problem too as he is holding a Columbian passport. We were always a couple of troubles and maybe those Chinese students as well. Our photography subject focused on renaissance architectures built by the famous *Galeazzo Alessi*. Claudio and I enjoyed that overnight trip with some the rest of the students. We stayed in a twenty-bedded hostel near the Tiber River and proximal to the *Piazza IV Novembre*. The group was grouped into two pairs so Claudio and I roamed around the town and compared some wonderful shots together. We were only asked to present twenty still shots, so we argued about the theme and came up with his own idea at the end. It was one of his majors so I gave way to his highness...as usual! Never argue with a Columbian drug dealer!

We finished at lunchtime and spent the afternoon in a small village called *Deruta*. An old man in a souvenir shop invited us for lunch in his house. We bought some little hand painted ceramics and pretended to be journalists from America. We arrived in a lovely Italian house in the village near his shop and his wife cooked a famous Etruscan dish with roasted salmon, courgettes and pesto linguine. It was deliciously washed down with a refreshing white wine drawn from a huge barrel in the house. We promised to take photos of them and feature it in a famous American magazine. After that scrumptious meal, we left the house laughing in tears.

"Due bambini…amore dolce dolce…il mio tesoro!!!" Our American accentuated-Italian worked and along the streets, we were taking the mickey out of the Italian couple. They were really keen to adopt us and feed us everyday as long as we make them famous and known in America and the world.

It was a hilarious, sunny afternoon. I looked forward to go back into the hostel and get ready for the class dinner with the rest of the group. Other students must be having a great time during that trip I reckoned. *Deruta* doesn't have a train station so we came by a taxi. Unfortunately, there wasn't any cab nor bus to take us back to *Perugia*. We stood at the terminal waiting for a lift. We were enjoying a huge cone of *fragola* and *tiramisu gelato*. Claudio and I were licking the dripping cone alternately and suddenly a white van came. It wasn't for hire but the Italian driver who barely spoke english stood out of the van and looked quite skeptical. Suddenly, a group of nuns arrived and jumped into the van. Someone came last and glanced at us.

"Are you going to the Basilica? Hurry, before they close!" The lady exclaimed.

She was wearing an all white habit and wimple as well as the rest. It was four of them and we both came along. I didn't have any idea where we're heading to? The van drove off as we were settling ourselves in our seats. The driver didn't say anything but just manoeuvred the car ridiculously as most Italians do. I heard that before and thought it was just a rumour but true. Claudio looked at me and gestured to shut up so I preferred and looked innocently.

"Have you been to *Assissi* before?" A nun seated in front turned her back and asked us with a strange, english accent.

"It's our first time, ma'am! We are doing some research in our school and my friend, Claudio is searching for his lost parents." Claudio replied and I was speechless. What does my lost parents have to do with *Assissi*?

"Where are you from?" Someone at the back added.

"We are students from London having a day trip in *Perugia*." I answered with some embarrassment.

The nuns looked Asian as they closely appeared. A bit like my Mama. They were all covered in white except their faces with rosary beads on their hands; very conservative too with their long sleeves, thick, white socks and black shoes.

"Where are you all originally from, if you don't mind me asking?" I looked each one of them and noticed the van moving uphill.

"We are nuns from the Assumption Convent of the Philippines. We were sent for a Catholic Mission, do you know?" The same lady from the front replied.

"My mother is Malaysian but I haven't been to Asia. Of course, we heard about the Philippines don't we, Claudio?"

"Yeah, definitely!"

Claudio trembled on his seat and seemed distracted. I was wondering what was he thinking that time?

"Of course, we have. It's the only Christian country in Asia that's why all of you guys are here? But thank you for the ride. God bless you all sisters!" He exclaimed.

We reached our destination as to my assumption after a journey along a snake road uphill. That gave me a headache next to the glasses of wines we had for lunch.

"We have arrived! Have a wonderful stay and we hope you will find what you're searching for. God bless you, children!" A nun stated in an old woman's voice. She looked more mature than the rest with the lines on her forehead and cheeks.

"Thank you so much sisters!"

We jumped out of the van and waited for the rest to come out completely. Claudio grabbed my arm and dragged me away.

"C'mon, dude! Let's get goin'."

I looked up and gazed on a church which seemed gothic to me. I had definitely no idea as I am not a Christian so maybe Claudio could give me some more information. We went inside and I saw paintings on the walls. Some of them have fallen down or were stripped off. The church looked very old. There was complete silence but I heard sounds of whispers. There weren't too many around but just us few scattered all over.

"This is the Basilica of St. Francis of Assissi. He is a patron saint of animals and the environment. He is buried downstairs on another church, do you know?"

Claudio whispered and sounded like he knew it very well.

"It's a gothic styled architecture as you may have seen from outside and inside. "

"Did you see those paintings on the walls, Lean?" He asked.

"They are works of Giotto and other Tuscan students in Rome. They were ruined by a strong earthquake but didn't completely destroy the church. They said there was a miracle that ceased it." He added and continued whispering and more in control of his voice gently.

Claudio was like a tour guide. Where did he get all those information if he said he hasn't been there at all? We went down and found another little church as well. In the middle, there was a fenced pillar and people lit candles around. Claudio pulled me near and I saw letters and photographs surrounding it.

"This is the tomb of St. Francis. This is where he was buried and the remains are still there! People offer prayers and write letters especially for those who are missing. According to the saint, the winds of nature will blow them back to where they belong. St. Francis will tame the wind and help you find them!"

"Pray, Lean! Your parents might be flown back, you'll never know."

That was utterly ridiculous! But to be honest, I had nothing to lose, do I? We had some silence as Claudio maybe offered some prayers, I don't know? He must have as he was born Catholic. I took my wallet out of my back pocket and opened it. I saw a photo of myself and my mama. It was the only picture I kept for so many years with me. Our faces have faded a bit from the heat and moisture expelled from my behind I guessed? Anyhow, St. Francis can help me look for my mama and also my baba which I included on my prayers. I wrote a little note just to make sure he won't forget the names of Suhaila and Jawad. I noticed, Claudio was roaming around the tall pillar and observing closely the letters and photos scattered around it. Some have came a long way and were down on their knees, in tears with so much faith to have answers to what they've been searching for. I looked around and realised that we have all came with one intention: longing for our loved ones to come back in our midst. Well, I wasn't intended to go to that place at all if not because of Claudio and those nuns.

I saw him on his knees, like the others. Claudio took something out of his pocket and it was the rosary beads used by Catholics for praying. He looked very serious and indestructible. He continued to pray in silence and never looked around nor thought about my presence. I remained standing in front of the others and felt the gravity pulling me down. I went on my knees and became infected by the others. Memories came back when I closed my eyes and my mama appeared right in front of me. She looked so beautiful in her white dress, smiling and ever so lovely. I prayed that one day, we would meet again and live in one home again. How I longed for her stories before I go to bed and her gentle embraces when I come home from school. I wanted my mama back…and my Baba? He can just be blown away forever and trapped and never come back! I hated him so much as he didn't treat me like his own…his son! Maybe I brought the right photo for St. Francis. I don't ever want to see my baba again and never have that fear inside me. His cruelty destroyed me and I will forever bear that in my life. This day has generated so much anger and that was all because of him. He was the father who obliterated a child's innocence and disrespected it. I just did right! I only want my mama back, so if the saint of God can do these miracles to others, then, please I deserve one miracle too!

"Let's go!"

Claudio tapped my shoulder and squeezed it lightly. I opened my eyes and saw him standing right next to me. He looked at me with compassion. I cried and I was completely out of myself on that occasion. He wiped my eyes with a moist tissue that felt like it was used before. He, then pulled me to stand up and gave me a hug.

"I know those tears, Lean."

"Your parents are looking at you now and can hear you crying out loud to be with them again."

"I can see so much faith in you. There's a perfect reason for anything and a right time for everything!"

We walked out of the church and the memories will only be on my thoughts to cherish forever. No photos were allowed so we only took them from the outside of the basilica. The skies were dimmed and the sunset prevailed. We witnessed a vast piece of the earth, overlooking the Umbria region. Claudio hired a green little Vespa to go down to the train station and we both jumped into it. It was a breezy evening and was an amazing experience for me. The night train back to the hostel wasn't too bad and we joined the rest of the group for a late supper.

We all ended pissed during that night and Claudio and I slept in one bed. No one really cared and neither did we. We flew back to London about midday, the following morning so the whole trip was purely educational, but for me, I made so much from it. Claudio remained calm and relaxed even during the flight. We flew with Ryanair from Perugia Airport to London Stansted. During the flight, I asked what Claudio was praying for when we went to that church and how did he knew all about it?

"My mom is a jetsetter and a devoted Catholic. She has always encouraged us to pray and go to church."

"I can always see her praying and holding a rosary everytime we travel and before she sleeps during the night."

Claudio and I were seated at the very back of the plane and he didn't really mind the cheap airline 'cos I knew, he must be an expensive traveller.

"I actually prayed for you, so you'd see your parents again, Lean."

"I am sorry that I brought you there but I admired how you respected other people's beliefs. You didn't turn me down."

Claudio looked at me and held my hand. It felt warm and soft like a child's. I didn't imagine someone could be so earnest like the way he was during the whole trip.

"I told you, things happen for great reasons and we never even planned to visit Assissi, did we?"

"I hope I made you happy but I respect if you didn't especially with your other belief and faith." He added.

"I am entirely delighted, Claudio. Thank you for bringing me to Assissi!" I answered.

He didn't know, a relief of anger was drawn out of me and still adhered to my nerves. I will never ever forget my Baba and forgiving him is still on my prayers and mostly on him too. His guilt should haunt him each night and regret that moment when he wounded my heart.

"You are so quiet there, Lean. Shall we look at our photos and start getting rid of the rubbish?"

"Yeah, but I will save all of them. I think they're all fab!" I replied and my attention was distracted from my heartbroken reminiscence.

Dearest Publisher,

I had a school trip to Perugia, Italy recently. It was basically for a photography project but Claudio and I ended up in Assissi. I realised how Catholics are very devoted and faithful to their belief in searching for a lost soul. Yeah, souls are like smoke that can be blown away and back to wherever they belong.

They kneeled down to their knees like we do and prayed solemnly and faithfully.

I wanted to go back and revise my prayers to be honest. I only prayed for my Mama and regret the entreaty for my Baba. I was filled with anger and hatred that time. St. Francis may grant my wish with a condition too, as I only want to have my Mama back and never my father again.

Sorry if I didn't include you in prayers but I was sure you weren't a lost soul anyway. I wish to catch up with you soon as we blow the readers of your writings.

The lost soul,

Assissi Boy

Chapetr Sixteen

The Eurostar train just left Avignon Centre Station in France. I was on that train heading back to London. It was a rainy, Sunday afternoon, sometime in March-last week I think? I spent a short weekend in Nice where Nasser had an annual conference meeting. I had to take a local train and changed to Avignon for Eurostar. Avignon Grand Centre Station was very modern with glass ceilings and very modern like a mini airport. It looked like a massive eskimo's hut but it was a stunning design by the *très grande vitesse* or the known TGV. The people coming in were all wet for the unexpected rain. I realised France isn't that far from England, hence, the unpredictable weather. It's thirteen degrees and quite cold especially on my out of weather attire. My fleece-lined woolen jacket was damped and cold so I took it off when I got inside the station. It was nice and warm for a start, then, hotter on my blue merino shirt. The EDF energy must be supplying them generously with superb heating. I took the shirt off and left a thin, grey t-shirt that I used the day before. It was enough really for a six-hour train journey back home.

Nasser was in a foul mood as the meeting went all about the legal implications and their responsibilities to the public and their consumers. There was a massive oil spill at the Gulf and it has affected their business directly. He knew I wasn't really interested but he mentioned it at bedtime and during breakfast so I noticed how greatly devastated he was. They are part supplier and financer so he must be very worried.

I stayed in a little bed and breakfast just outside Nice's city centre, Mont Boron. He came and stayed for a couple of hours for the last two nights but still went back to his posh hotel room with some other colleagues. I was used to this arrangement and never did I ever complain at all. I just enjoyed the English Riviera and it was my first time so I had a look around and took plenty of photos for my projects in school.

Nasser asked me one of those nights, "When was the last time when you were ever so happy, *habibi*?"

"Today!" I answered with so much excitement and put a big smile on my face.

"Thank you for everything! With you, my dreams are coming true!"

Nasser smiled back with a little frown and looked a bit puzzled. We were lying naked in bed with just a white sheet covering our waists and below. We did fit on that single bed on my cheap hotel but we were fine.

"How's uni?"

"I heard you're doing well and not far to go?"

"Time is really quick!"

He was like a parent to me, asking me all these personal questions and knowing all my whereabouts. I have been so open to him except my relationship with Claudio. That subject, I'd have to keep to myself! I don't think he will be happy hearing that, nor, approve to it. I can just imagine how can he be in rage, although, I haven't seen him so upset at all. I have always pleased him and followed his guidance. I kept asking myself, until when am I going to be attached to this person? Sometimes, I feel guilty that he might think of me just using him and his power? Well, he uses me too for his pleasure.

"When I finish university, I want to stay in London and find a decent job. But I assume, that is impossible as I will be in breach of contract to my benefactors, isn't it?" I looked at him and saw he's closed his eyes but suddenly opened.

"On the other hand, I have responsibilities to my countrymen. Also, I want to find my parents and make them proud of what I have achieved." I added.

"That's a really noble idea. Well, you can gain some work experiences and make a proposal or project that you will implement for the youth in Yemen."

Nasser verbalised in a sleepy voice. It was two in the morning and he will be off for a meeting at eight. He must be really tired after finishing a long day of discussion and ending the day-jiggy jiggy with me? He was fit like a horse at his age and maybe the same when he's with women too. I never asked!

"Honey, you must be tired? I'll get you a taxi to drive you back in your hotel, ok?"

I pulled myself up and looked for the telephone. He rose up and started gathering his clothes thrown all over the little hotel room. He moved really slow, and seemed not bothered.

"Family is so important and they are the people who will never leave you!"

"Always remember that!"

I saw him and just wondered how he got into his shirt and trousers so quickly! He is so used to this dressing up and keeping himself up and running.

"Never leave me?" I asked and put the phone down.

"So where are they now if they didn't leave me on own, alone all this time?"

I was trying to shout but just whispered with a harsh voice.

"Leandro, your parents only want the best for you and they didn't leave you. *Inshallah,* you will reunite with them but you have a duty to honor and respect your parents. Don't tell me, you forgot what the prophets have said?"

Nasser looked around and checked that he's got everything. He kissed me on my forehead and just left. Well, he's damn right as usual. Just take it from an old man or a messenger of a prophet for heaven's sake! Anyway, I still have time to go out and discover Nice's nightlife. It must be interesting on a Friday night with some French guys, huh?

I went out that night and I only had some few pints of Stella. The crowd was a mixture of French and Italian but very interesting. I wasn't really up for anything that night. Quite unusual but just plenty of stuffs messing around my brains. I didn't stay long but it was nice to see the nightlife in Nice. It's not really a known gay venue to be honest. I wished Claudio was there too, coached me on photography and went out with me. Impossible…impossible…

The train just left Gare du Nord, Paris. Another three hours of train journey, but I was quite comfy at the edge of this economy seat. Paris was dry and there was hardly any rain. Plenty of passengers jumped into the carriages, yet, I was still on my own on this four-seater square. I placed my small luggage above on the rail and hanged my jacket on the side. It must have dried by now. I thought the train wasn't too bad with the time and speed. How amazing! Whoever invented the Eurostar is such a genius.

Nasser has never invited me abroad in any of his conferences but that weekend in Nice was a blessing in disguise. Again, I enjoyed my visa card with Nasser's permission. He pays for it but I never abuse it. I can't still imagine spending other people's money, so I always send him the billing statement even he doesn't ask for it.

Did he really mean to bring me there just to remind me about my parents or again, for his convenience? I always knew this guy would do things with rationale but somehow, I thanked him for that little trip. T'was an ecstacy indeed where I found an answer to my longtime uncertainty. It was a thrilling experience of a lifetime apart from the great scenery and the joys of being with *habibi*.

Finally, the train has reached St. Pancras, London! It's almost midnight so I rushed to catch the last trip of the Picadilly line going home to Knightsbridge as my final destination. My jacket has really dried after all that heating on the train for six hours. I realised my earphones were stucked in my ears with the music on but my mind has been diverted to the lovely weekend I had and how it came to an end. It's school time and can't wait to see Claudio again in the afternoon. He will be shocked if I tell him how divine my trip was with the lovely Nasser in Nice? All he knew about him was a dedicated foster parent. That's all!

London was colder that night. Around twelve degrees I guessed. I walked all the way through from South Kensington Station to the flat on a quiet side-lighted street along the posh mansions. Everyone must be in bed preparing for business at the start of the week-typical Londoners! The flat looked so empty and dark from afar. I opened the black door as I helplessly carried my bag and took my jacket off. There were plenty of letters from the post for the past two days. They scattered on the floor and I just knelt and gathered them one by one. I wasn't bothered reading those at that time of the day, was I? I headed off to my bedroom and left my bag and jacket on the sofa.

"I will deal with them whenever!"

I went straight to my bedroom and took off my clothes. I felt chilly and realised the heating must be switched on. I was dragged into bed and slept like a log. Just a few hours and I have to be ready for school. I wrapped myself with a cold duvet and left the study lamp on towards me to heat me up a little bit. Well, that was the end of the day and a new one will start soon!

Dear Mr. Publisher,

I just spent a fantastic weekend in the English Riviera, France.

I have attached all the necessary events that maybe of relevance for your reference.

It's a beautiful part of the south of France. Guess what? I think I can live there quite soon if destiny permits. Language will be the only barrier but that is way too easy and would be lovely to speak French!

How are you anyway?

You must come up to London and we have lunch as usual. I missed our laughs and you talking about your grumpy wife-making conversations with her pills. She must be getting mad like you? I am only joking, Kevin.

I really hope to see you soon mate!

I will be coming back to Nice in summer with great stories for sure!

The beach is way so cool to swim and the seafood salad is delicious!

Take care,

Your Famous Writer

Chapter Seventeen

"I'm already here upstairs, Kevin!" I yelled as I dropped my phone on a white cloth covered table at the Tower 42 in London. It's at the tallest, Natwest Tower and the restaurant by the famous Gary Rhodes. I have been there twice and I loved the ambiance and the food was just amazing!

Kevin spent the whole day in Liverpool Street for a conference workshop at the Royal Publisher's Guild. It was a Wednesday evening and the people present in the restaurant were quite a handful. Everyone was taking their time and didn't mind the rush hour outside the business capital of the city.

I was sitting down in a two-seater table overlooking the Gherkin and the Tower of London. It was almost eight in the evening of the last days somewhere in February. I can't remember exactly but I was sure, the temperature was freezing out in the streets of London that time. I just had the last sip of a glass of red wine from the house whilst waiting for Kevin. It was a nice evening catching up with him really after not having visited West Sussex for ages. I had a lazy day and my class finished early so I went home and changed to my dinner jacket.

Kevin just suddenly appeared right in front of me without me noticing him.

"Hello, gorgeous!" He exclaimed and kissed me on my forehead.

I hugged him and he smelled really nice, like an evening perfume. He was wearing a pink shirt, white tie and underneath a dark blue jacket. He looked really smart!

"Hey, mister! How's your day been?" I asked and stood up at the same time.

"Really, good! Not too bad so far, really." He answered and took off his jacket and hanged it at the back of his chair. Kevin sat down and placed his phone on the table too and looked at me with a gentle grin.

"And how are you, Lean?"

He stared at me from head and down, taking note of the way I looked that evening. I was wearing a simple cream shirt in silk and a light blue, glossy jacket. I wore it last during a dinner party in college not long ago. I loved the comfort of wearing that suit and how elegance it looked, yet, very simple. Kevin actually bought it for me from Burberry in New Bond Street. It was a late Christmas present but I really loved it.

"So, have you fancied anything yet to order? I am starving and we had an early Chinese lunch today. I only had coffee this afternoon, so maybe I'll have a steak. What are you having?"

He was flicking at the menu whilst muttering at me without looking.

"I'll try the pheasant, actually." I replied with certainty to have that dish. I haven't had pheasant for ages and I usually have them when I spend lunch with him out in the countryside.

Kevin called the attendant and ordered the food we have agreed. I left everything to the person paying for dinner that night.

"How's school and yourself? Is your *habibi* treating you well? Kevin began to ask me all these questions, updating himself about me.

I was always open to him and talked everything about me and Nasser. It's not a kept secret really. He listened to me and understood like he has experienced my life himself. He always made sure that I have everything that I needed in school and at home. He was just like a father to me. He also knew everything about Claudio and how I loved being a single and young gay man living in London.

"You look so chic tonight, Mr. Al Bahir! Guys should be running after you tonight in Soho!" He teased as he rolled up his sleeves up and repositioned himself slowly on his chair.

We were shared a bottle of red wine just before the food arrived and in fact, nearly finished it and ordered another one for our meal. It was a great night just catching up and finishing a long day gently with a sumptuous food and wine and a wonderful company. Sandra was left in their house in Tunbridge Wells. She wasn't a London person and would prefer to stay at home or being in a quiet environment. It was a two-day event so Kevin stayed in a hotel near the conference venue. That night went really quick and we enjoyed our food and never doubted them anyway. Part of our conversations was our years in Sana'a. We reminisced my life in school and how I met my long, lost German guy- Juergen. We were laughing as Kevin mocked about it. We also giggled about his wife's frustration to come back to England in desperation. Sandra didn't like Yemen. It was hot and dirty for her and the people were so uneducated according to her. She preferred to stay in their apartment and prepared their own food as she hated eating Arabic food elsewhere. She loved the Indian food though and invited some of the students' parents to cook for her in their apartment whilst she supervised food hygiene and handling. We had a laugh!

I didn't plan to go anywhere else that night as I would be fine with Kevin. I preferred to go home and just get ready for school the following day. It was almost eleven at night and we decided to leave. We finished two bottles of French red wine and indulged ourselves with a white chocolate fudge brownie in warm caramel sauce. It was delectable! Before we left, I went down to the bathroom to tidy myself up. Kevin waited for me just at the reception wearing his long, grey coat and thick scarf. I was feeling tipsy and really can't wait to go to bed. I could still hear the loud music from the restaurant on the way to the loo and as I entered, the room was quite dim and subtle. My eyes straightly caught two men kissing just behind the booth. I wasn't surprised initially but was dreadfully shocked seeing Claudio kissing another guy! They were on their formal clothes too so I hardly recognised Claudio.

"Claudio?" I whispered gently and hesitantly. I still couldn't believe it was him.

They both stopped and looked at me. It was really Claudio! The other guy looked a bit older than us I thought. He looked oriental with his fair skin and Chinese looking eyes. I was so stunned.

"Who is he, babe?" The Asian guy asked him.

"He's a friend from school. A really nice friend!" Claudio replied.

I was speechless and both of them came towards me.

"Leandro, this is Choy Chan. Choy, meet Leandro, my Arab friend!"

We shook hands and I was still frozen and astounded where I was standing. Claudio didn't say they were boyfriend or friend but I definitely saw them kissing right in front of me. He even had the nerve to introduce me as his friend, so what the hell was I doing there?

"Nice to me meet you and lovely to see you guys! I really have to go. See you later!" I rushed myself out of the room and felt like being squeezed in between by two hard walls. I felt my chest so tight and unable to breathe. I quivered in tears as I walked near Kevin. He was very keen to go and as he looked at me, his face began to wonder. I didn't care how I looked like but I was definitely devastated after being in that scene.

"Leandro, is everything alright?" Kevin asked with a huge concern.

"Let's go please, hurry!" I answered in a low voice and felt more like crying.

I grabbed my coat but didn't wear it. I was feeling really warm and clothes felt really tight, strangling me. I dragged Kevin to the nearest lift, it was open and waiting for passengers. I pressed ground floor firmly with my cold and wobbly fingers. The door closed and I felt my knees soft and numb.

"What the hell is wrong with you?"

Kevin came closer to me and held both of my shoulders and began shaking me. I fell on the floor and cried. I held my voice and just mumbled but cried out loud at the end. Kevin kneeled in front of me and still waited for me to say something.

"I hate him! I fucking hate you, Claudio!!!"

I screamed in tears and lost control of myself. Kevin hugged me really tight and stroked my back.

"Shhh…Calm down, Lean! Calm down. Tell me please, what's wrong? Shhh…"

I was still wobbling in tears until we reached the ground floor. The lift opened and Kevin gave way to let me out first. He grabbed my coat and held me on my left shoulder.

"I'll take you home." He uttered gently.

"It's ok. I'll be fine, Kevin." I replied and wiped the tears in my face with my sleeves.

"No, let's get a cab and I'll take you back home, ok?" He insisted and went out of the building. He hailed a black cab just in front of the rotating door. I saw him as I waited inside. He was talking to the driver and seemed like giving him direction or maybe negotiating, I don't know. I still felt really hot despite the cold weather coming inside the door. I saw Kevin waving at me to go out. I got into the cab and he followed me. He banged the door and got rid of our coats.

"Knighstbridge then, please!" He yelled with a deep voice.

He was really taking me home.

"Kevin, honestly, I could go home on my own. Can we just drop you in your hotel. You should go to bed early, c'mon!" I persevered for the last time just in case he would give up.

"Lean, I am taking you home so just calm down and we will get there soon." He verbalised with a loud voice that time.

It didn't take long and we reached Knightsbridge. The cab stopped right in front of the gate and I saw the house covered in darkness. I could still picture it out from far with its white paint and two huge pillars right in front of a spectacular building in Chelsea. I stepped out of the flat and searched for the keys on my jacket. I left Kevin in the cab but he was quick and I heard the taxi moved away swiftly. I opened the door and didn't care to switch the lights on but the poor man did it. I ran straight to the bathroom and knelt in front of the toilet sink. I felt the urge to throw up!

"Ughhh...This is unfair! I am just a stupid idiot!"

I vomited an awful lot of red bits and pieces. It must be a combination of pheasant and red wine but don't forget the pudding too. I felt my gut was turning upside down. Kevin came near me and flushed the sink. I was startled a bit and he stroked my back again. I felt a little better; quite comfortable with his gentle strokes and at the same time relieved after all the stuffs caming out out of my system.

"Shhh…Come on, let's hit the sack. It is very late and you need to be up early." Kevin assisted me to get up and walked with me to my bed. He took off my clothes and laid them on the floor. I was left with just my underwear. I laid myself down in bed and he covered me with the duvet. I felt warm enough and my head really heavy weighted. I slumbered myself like a log but deep inside was still a crying voice of a brokenhearted Lean.

I woke up and felt the weight of my head taking me down on the floor. I haven't forgotten what happened that night. I stepped into the hot shower and cried again. I was deeply hurt. I didn't know what to do with Claudio if I'd ever see him again. Avoiding him might help me move on and just get on with my life! I realised, Kevin was gone and I had no idea when he left me. He must have gone back to his hotel room late that night or left in the early morning?

The morning class seemed useless. I didn't understand any of it, nor, remembered what happened that morning gone? I headed to the library instead as I wasn't feeling hungry for lunch. It was extremely quiet and not many students around. There was nothing for me to research or study, so I took out my diary and thought of writing some bad news on it. I was sitting down at the very end corner of the room. The shelves surrounding me were filled with thousands of books upto the ceiling. There was a computer on the desk but I wasn't tempted to use it. I opened my diary and looked for a blank page. Half of the book was empty as I don't really use it a lot except for some very memorable occasions that I should take note of.

I didn't know how to start and what to write. I knew it was a sad story but I thought maybe not to record it. It'll only remind me of another miserable chapter of my life. I wanted to express that very emotional situation, so yes, why not write it down to an old friend who has been always there. I looked at the blank page. It was clean and blank entirely, waiting for some stains of ink.

"Hey, I knew I will find you here!"

It was a voice that I genuinely recognised. Claudio stood behind me without my knowing. I turned my back and he was there attempting to surprise me. It wasn't very funny at all. I wasn't ready to face nor talk to him that day or ever!

"Let's go for coffee, c'mon. My treat!" He yelled in a low voice.

I remained speechless and didn't know what to do. As if nothing happened last night and Claudio stayed exactly the same. He grabbed my hand and pulled me up. I placed all my stuffs in the bag and walked out of the library with him. We went to the Italian café where we usually hang out for an afternoon food and coffee. It wasn't busy on that Thursday, just after midday. Claudio went ahead to our favorite two-seater table at the bottom end of the restaurant where we would always sit and spend lunch together. I was still very silent. He called the young Italian lady who knew us and so she replied with our usual orders. We loved their lasagna and Sicilian lemonade. Also, followed with two double shots of espresso.

"Claudio, about last night?" I asked in a low voice and not looking at him.

"Yeah, Lean. What about it? Where you jealous with Choy? Uyyyy...." He laughed.

"He is the guy from my other class, kinda cute, isn't he?"

I suddenly felt the heat went up my spine and into my head. I was full of anger that time and I wanted to slap him so hard. I was so annoyed by his attitude. What the hell was he thinking? I controlled myself and tried to be calm and civilised.

"Claudio, you and I are going out together and I saw you kissing another guy last night? What the fuck do you think should I do?" I looked at him and cried. I felt so numb and my face really red.

"You came to see me now and looked like nothing happened? I can't believe you!"

I was crying more but I forced myself to refrain from becoming too aggressive and loud. His facial expression changed and realised how serious and hurt I was. I didn't manage to hide my feelings as I was very upset and really disgusted.

"Lean, listen. Choy is one of the guys I go out with, too. I like him the way I like you and there wasn't any commitment? We were all young boys having fun, aren't we?" He remained calm as he looked at me in the eyes.

He attempted to hold my hands but I refused. I was shocked with what he said and felt my chest really tight and my ribcage holding me to breathe.

"This is very disconcerting and you just break my heart, Claudio! You know I am in love with you and why are you hurting me this way? You are breaking my heart!"

"You really just fucking did!"

I wanted to scream out loud but my breathing became more difficult and seemed I was going to collapse where I was seated from. I cried more tears and sounded breathless. I didn't know what to do or say anymore and was totally distressed.

"I like you too, Lean. But I didn't promise you anything, did I? You are a very nice guy but this is who I am and I thought you were the same too? We seem to enjoy each other's company and I don't mind you seeing other guys even. It's part of being young!"

Claudio was incredibly shocking and I didn"t believe he thought the same way for me. I felt the whole place was squeezing me in between and I was running out of air. I stood up and ran away from him. There was nothing left for me to say and everything was clear. He played on my feelings and I was just an old fool, believing a stupid guy like him!

I was trotting along Regent's park and didn't know where to go. I was crying my heart out and suffered the pain inside my heart. I despised him and didn't wish to see him anymore! Claudio was just another person who let me down again. He was like my father who never cared nor respected me.

I ended up going home that afternoon and missed the rest of my classes. I needed someone to embrace and comfort me. How I wished my Mama was there to hold me in her arms or even someone who would stand by me. I was all alone and suffered the pain on my own.

Claudio once said, "everything happens for a reason and things happen at the right time." What does he mean by that? What good reason was there after he broke my heart and it what a perfect timing when I saw him kissed another guy?

Dearest Kevin,

I bet it's not new anymore of you seeing me being brokenhearted.

Yes, another man whom I believed would be so genuine and forever this time-but I was wrong. He was just the same like those two before who failed me and left me in the end.

I am so hurt and feeling down and lonely. I feel the world has turned away from me.

Thank you so much for bringing me home that night, sir. I really do appreciate it.

To be honest, I really wanted to cry out loud and suffer more pain but it seemed there hasn't left for me to tear for. Life has brought me so much challenges after all these years and I have grown so much stronger. I don't regret them all as part of my fate and I look ahead in the future with more courage and confidence.

Lessons that I have learned?

"Things happen for a very good reason."

So I shouldn't waste no time and make the most of what tomorrow brings.

Thank you so much Mr. Fitzgerald!

Yours truly,

Mr. Al Habir

Chapter Eighteen

A post from the bank addressed to me. It was from the Lloyds TSB Bank Plc.

I wasn't banking with them and I never contacted them for any financial reason or whatsoever?

I opened the letter and it was an invitation to see the bank's financial adviser.

That was strange?

I rang the number written on the letter and booked for a Saturday appointment. There was none available and I was advised to come to the bank ASAP for an important matter!

"Please don't say I was a victim of fraud or anything fishy? I can't have a loan anymore or maybe I could transfer my student loan for a low interest or a cashback?"

They promised it won't take too much of my time as I had classes in that afternoon.

I hurriedly went to the Lloyds TSB in Knightsbridge just along the Brompton Road. It was quite busy and packed. I went inside the bank and it wasn't that big at all. There was a long queue towards the cashiers but I approached the lady on the information desk. A tiny lady with very thin, grey hair looked at me and smiled.

"Good afternoon! How can I help you today?" She asked with a beam and enthusiasm.

She was wearing a white stripy top and I saw her name badge. Her name was Caroline. Caroline Stephenson-Lloyds TSB Plc.

"Hi, Caroline! How are you?"

"I received a letter from the bank and have come for an appointment." I replied.

"Is it Leandro Al Bahir?"

"Yes, that's me!"

"If you could bear with me, I'm going to call my colleague. Just give me five secs."

She left me and went inside a coded door. I waited. I looked at my watch and it was quarter to two in the afternoon. I was suppose to have a class at three thirty that day hoped it wouldn't take long.

I saw Caroline walking towards me on her mini skirt and a short guy was following behind her.

"Mr. Al Bahir, this is Toby. He will be able to help you, ok?"

"Sure, thank you." I answered and I became more curious.

"Hi Mr. Al Bahir, I'm Toby! Will you come with me, please."

He was a short English man, with curly hair and thick eyeglasses.

He led me and went inside a little private room with glass walls and blinds surrounded. There was a small desk with a black desktop computer and a brown folder on the table.

"Sit down, please."

"How are you? Can I call you Leandro?" He asked.

"Yes, of course. I am very well, thank you!"

"I have some afternoon classes and I have to be in school before thirty past three."

"What is it all about? Can you tell me?"

We both sat down and he opened the brown folder and took a sheets of paper. He gave them to me.

"Mr. Nasser Al Sadeq left these for you. If you want to have a look and accept them, please. That would be great!"

I took the paper and read what was written on them.

Nasser put myself as the owner of his flat in Chelsea.

"That's the place where I live?"

Also, there was a savings fund of one million pounds to be transferred to my account subject to my identifiable sugnatures.

It was a formal will, signed by him and a solicitor.

"What's all of these? Can you explain?" I asked with so much astonishment.

"I am sorry for your loss, sir." He replied.

"Loss? What? What do you mean? I don't understand what you're talking about?"

"Mr. Al Sadeq has passed away last weekend, didn't you know, sir?"

"That is not true! We were together last week in France!"

"I don't understand. I can't believe this!"

"Are you having a laugh?"

I became hysterical and sobbed in tears. I searched for my phone and tried to ring him but his phone was off.

"Nasser, where are you?"

"I am sorry, Leandro. I thought you already knew. Sorry, sir."

He placed his hand on my shoulder and it wasn't enough to calm me down.

I was totally stunned and nearly collapsed on my chair.

"What am I supposed to do now?"

"This is not so true! Please tell me, you're lying!" I screamed and my eyes flooded with tears. I wiped them with my hands and my nose was dribbling too.

"This letter was in his safe in this bank."

"The American Bank in Yemen sent us a copy of his death certificate and advised to close all of his accounts."

"Here's my business card, sir."

"Call me if you need any other information on your accounts."

"I am deeply sorry, again! Sorry."

He assisted me out of the room and walked with me upto the entrance of the bank.

I was still in tears and as I walked along the pavements of the Brompton Road, I didn't notice anything or anyone along the way. It was meant to be a busy afternoon but I felt just on my own in the streets, in tears, lonely and heartbroken.

I didn't know where to go? Definitely not at home!

I would just remember Nasser as I stroll around the flat!

"Why did he die and I didn't even have a clue or anything? I should definitely find out why?"

"I need him and I love him so much!"

"I couldn't live without him!"

"He is my everything and he's all that I need!"

I wished someone would pinch me that afternoon. It was a hell of a nightmare!

I missed my afternoon and evening classes. I have lost the will to live and wished I was dead too!

It was a question of why all of my loved ones leave me without a hint? I was like a child left in the middle of a motorway not knowing what to do.

Dear Kevin,

Nasser is dead!

I am not sure if you have known but I was utterly shocked by this very sad news!

I hadn't had a clue until his bank called me gave me a will that was signed by him.

He left me and that was the last thing I thought about him.

I still have to find out how he died. I can't think of any health problems that he may have suffered or was he killed or murdered? I don't know…

I will never find someone like him.

Someone who will inspire me and encourage me to achieve more!

I really do not know what to do now or how am I start to pick up the pieces again?

I need you, Kevin! You're the only one who's left to look after me.

I need all the strength to carry on and fulfill my dreams.

I wish to see you soon, please?

Lonely,

Lean

Chapter Nineteen

"Is this Leandro Al Bahir?"

"Yes, it's him! Who's that?"

"My name is Lenny, I am a nurse from Chelsea and Westminster Hospital in London."

She sounded really calm over the phone. A nurse from a hospital was calling me for what?

"Sir, I would like to inform you that your partner Claudio is in intensive care unit at the moment. He is asking if you could to come and see him!" She added.

"Why? What happened? What is going on with him?" I was totally astounded.

I didn't know what to do.

"He was not my partner in the first place as far as I'm aware!"

"Ok, tell him that I am on my way! Bye!"

The adrenaline rushed above my head. I don't know why? What happened to Claudio? I haven't spoken to him for months nor seen him in school? What has he done to himself and why is he in the hospital? Intensive care unit?

I knew where the hospital is. It is my local hospital too, although I haven't been there as a patient so far. I just kept on seeing it by passing Fulham Road. I changed my pyjamas into a pair of black jeans and grabbed a blue denim jacket. I took a black cab and directed the driver to the hospital. It only took about ten minutes. It was a chilly Sunday night. My feet were cold. I was just wearing a pair of leather sandals. I jumped out of the cab in front of the hospital. The taxi meter charged me seven pounds but I gave the driver a tenner and never looked back. I rushed to the reception and asked where the intensive care unit was? It was on the fifth floor of the building. I haven't been inside that hospital before. It wasn't like a hospital building. It was merely painted in white with glasses everywhere so the atmosphere looked bright and clear. The lift was very slow and I wished I could have flown wherever Claudio was. There was a clear direction were the unit was. I went in directly and the door was closed and no one could easily get in. There was a buzzer. I rang and a voice came up.

"Hi, can I help you!"

"I came to visit Claudio! Claudio Rodriguez?"

"Come in!"

I heard a snap on the door and I assumed it was unlocked. I pushed it and I was able to get in. I was walking rapidly and as I got into the unit, there were beds lined with other patients. There were machines attached to them that I don't have any idea what were they all about?. It made me felt more anxious and I was so overwhelmed! I hardly recognised Claudio. He was on a bed at a corner end. He has a mask on his face. He looked at me and looked so poignant.

"What happened to you? Bloody hell! What is this?" I shouted in tears.

There wasa machine beside him playing up with blood. I don't understand!

"It's ok, Lean. I am fine!"

"Hi there, I'm Lenny!"

"I rang you earlier. Are you Leandro?"

A short, Asian lady approached me.

"Yes, I am Leandro!"

"What's wrong with him?"

Claudio took off the mask covering his face and sighed deeply.

"Lenny, let me explain to him. Thank you for calling him!"

The nurse offered me a chair and left slowly.

I didn't think of sitting down so I came near Claudio. There was a tube on his neck connected to the machine and I can see the lines filled with blood.

"I am on dialysis machine. It is washing my blood from all the toxins. You sit down, Lean."

"What is going on Claudio?"

"I have had problems of sleeping lately and I asked for some sleeping tablets from the GP. They were rubbish so I drank them all in one go. I didn't realise it was too much until I was found unconscious at the school library."

"What? You are mad!"

"You know I am!"

"Thank you for coming, Lean! Very much appreciated."

"I didn't know who to call aside from you, honestly."

Claudio looked down and started rubbing his hands. He had two other needles in his arms. He was dressed in a blue hospital gown. I can't believe seeing him like that. There was a monitor behind him with different colors and numbers and they kept on alarming on and off-in different tunes! It was my first time in hospital. In intensive care unit!

"Claudio I want you to know that…"

"Lean, I called for you not because of all these drama. I have made some huge mistakes and I regret it!"

"Forgive me, please?"

He held my hand. His hands were cold. He was holding mine firmly and I can't let go easily.

"Claudio!"

"Lean, I am leaving next week!"

"I will continue my studies in Florida."

"My student visa has expired and I doubt that they would renew it as I wasn't doing well in school."

"I can't be bothered!"

"I just want to say goodbye to you."

"I want to leave but not without seeing you!"

"Well, here I am!"

"You can see and feel me now!"

My voice sounded a bit shaky and I cried. I didn't want to cry just because of that stupid guy who cheated and played on me.

Damn, I cried in front of him!

He didn't deserve it! But I guess I was just being true to myself and to Claudio.

He has been such a part of me since I came to England.

"I am sorry to hear you leaving."

"But goodbyes may not be forever!"

"I wish you all the best, Claudio. I really do!"

"Thank you for being such a special part of me and I will never ever forget the day we met and so as today!"

His eyes were filled with tears but he remained silent.

"There's my watch on that drawer, if you can hand it to me please."

I opened the drawer and saw a silver and gold watch. I gave it to him.

"Take this as a silly remembrance from me."

"I have nothing else to give you now, so."

"Oh no, don't worry! You don't have to do this, no!"

"Lean, this watch will always remind you of me, everytime you look at the time."

"It will tell you over and over that time is running even when you lose track on it but it will also help you back on track-on time!"

Claudio placed the watch on my left palm and helped me grasp it firmly.

I nodded and kissed him on his forehead. It was clammy. He had a steam from the oxygen mask and my lips were wet and tasted a bit salty. I smelt a faded perfume from his hair. I missed him but the time has come to let go.

"Thank you, Claudio."

"Thank you!"

"You know where to find me if you need anything!"

"Take care and goodbye!"

I walked away from him gently and another lady in blue uniform approached me.

"Sir, can I speak to you quickly please?"

"Sure!" I replied as I wiped the tears soaking my eyes. I felt so embarrassed.

She handed me a box of tissues.

"Thank you!"

"My name is Laura, I'm the sister-in charge. We can sit down at the relative's waiting room. Let me take you there."

"Sure!" I was sniffing my nose and recomposed myself for a bit.

We sat in front of each other in a small room just outside the unit and she handed me a survey paper to be filled up and a business card. The room was really tiny and dark with a stiff, blue sofa. It was a waiting area for people who wanted to see their loved ones on those hospital beds.

She took more contact details from me and would like to call me just in case if Claudio needed me or maybe them too. I thought it was fine. She offered more help with anything else but I guessed some little information about Claudio were enough to fill me in.

I left the hospital and chose to walk back home. It wasn't that far at all to walk back to Knightsbridge. It was around two in the morning and Fulham Road seemed quiet with a few cars passing through. The street lights and traffic bulbs were the ones left awake, enlightening the chilly atmosphere.

I took the watch from my jacket pocket and looked at it. It was a Cartier in gold and silver. I saw Claudio wearing it before and I really liked it. I remembered mentioning it to him when I first saw him wearing it. I really fancied his Cartier watch. It was a Roadster by Cartier in an 18 carat gold and silver. Yes, it looked a bit old as there were scratches all over that fancy timepiece, but, the thought counted really so much.

He was right.

Time is essential and it's important to be reminded of it to keep us back on track, in time!

"I will wear it everyday, Claudio."

"I will keep myself on track and on time."

"I will waste no time and there's no point of turning back!"

"Farewell, Claudio. Goodbye!"

Dearest Publisher,

It's cold and damp outside this very early morning.

I had a short sleep but prior to that, I went to see an old friend…an old special someone in hospital.

Claudio.

He had an overdose and was in intensive care unit!

Don't react ye,t but listen, he wanted me to come and say goodbye as he will be moving abroad.

Yes, he will be totally far away and the two of us will stay in the past forever…   I hope! He wished me well and I did the same thing, too.

He actually gave me a reminder of him. He gave me his Cartier watch that I really fancied, the first time I met him.

I will show it to you, don't worry.

I thought that was very sweet of him but the lesson there being was about time.

Time to let go of the past and time to look forward for the future!

Time that I will no longer waste and guess what? It's time for me to prepare for school today!

Have a lovely time wherever you are today!

See you later!

Lean xxx

Chapter Twenty

If I only realised that Nasser was undergoing through so much, then, I would have never made him more worried about me. Never should have I demanded many other favours from him but served and made him more proud of me.

But he has gone and his death, I felt so guilty about. He passed away in a non- inevitable way that traumatised my well being!

"I have so many questions for you, *habibi.*"

"You always reminded me to be tough and strong and not stupid!"

"But what did you do to yourself? What have you done?"

"Should you be ashamed of yourself and shall I be embarrassed of your failure?"

"I can't believe you have done this to me?"

Nasser Al Sadeq's body was found in the shores of Hodeidah, Yemen and could hardly be identified. His corpse was deemed to have been in the seawater for a longwhile. He was very swollen but all intact. He died in respiratory arrest due to drowning and nothing else so far. There was no any other signs of assault nor involvement of drugs.

Nasser was cremated straight away and no family was ever in contact at all. He hasn't left any letters nor signs of his misery. His death was never expected nor anticipated.

Jubail Oil was in a dilemma after having all the accusations regarding the oil leak found at the Arabian Gulf. It has affected most countries in the Middle East and the United Nations has released a resolution to shut the oil producer and all networks held accountable for.

It was very tragic as Europe and Asia have frozen their demands and changed their suppliers to prevent them from being involved in the cold case. Stockholders and directors have left and never been seen, soon after.

The worst part was the huge company's responsibility for the damages caused in communities and individuals that have lost their livelihoods and given them health problems. It was like a flood of plague along the Arabian seas.

It was a foreseen global disgrace and those responsible for it would have to pay the highest cost! Death wasn't even enough to forfeit the price!

The oil company that was in a huge turmoil claimed that it was the reason why Nasser ended his life. He had alcohol intoxication and drowned himself on the Red Sea. They can't figure out any foul play nor other motives for his death. They must be bloody joking me! Or were those guys having a laugh?

Nasser was a completely opposite man and that wasn't the way I knew him! He could never do that to himself. He's the toughest guy I have ever known!

"Nasser, wherever you are right now, please make a way and prove them wrong?"

"You inspired and encouraged me to become the best person that everyone can be proud of especially my family and my country. Look at you now? You couldn't even speak up and stand up to defend yourself?"

"I don't know what to feel and say, *habibi.* You have always made me proud and encouraged to do better and not just a mediocre. Listen to you?"

"Look who's talking now?"

"You made me believe that life's a test and we could all survive and make it happen?"

"I only pray that you will still be the person who loved me and enlightened my future ahead. That will never change, Nasser."

"I want to be proud of you and continue to look up on you but I am not sure now. I felt embarrassed that you have been weak too and didn't fight for yourself and showed others that they're wrong?"

"Rest in peace, *habibi*. In the midst of *Allah*. I love you so much."

"I will never ever forget you and will always remain in my thoughts and your words of wisdom will always be cherished!"

"I love you and I will see you in due time!"

Chapter Twenty One

"I am catching the train at 2120h to Paris!" I exclaimed as I stood at the middle of the St. Pancras Station, London.

It was calm and quiet on a Tuesday night. The London's rush hour has passed and the Eurostar passengers were less than a handful even on the economy seats. My left shoulder was holding a blue rucksack; quite bulky but light. A half–bitten Cornish pasty was on a grasp by my left hand and a large soya latte being gripped on my opposite hand.

As I continued talking, I remained holding my phone in between my right shoulder and ear tightly. I was wearing a beige linen top, quite crumpled yet it really suited my dark, olive skin. I looked thin with a skinny and chocolate linen trousers paired with a pair of brown, leathered Gucci slippers.

"I am off to France just to unwind but I will keep in touch! I won't be long, I just need a break from reality!" I grinned as he laid my bag on an empty seat opposite to my designated chair. I dropped my food and drink on the table and just let go of the phone into the comfy train seat. I remained standing and untangled a red merino jumper tied on my waist. I closed my eyes slowly and took a deep breath feeling all the exhaustion embedded along my spine. It has been an immensely challenging week and at the back of my mind, I have done so much but on the other hand, the waiting has gone adieu. My eyes suddenly opened wide with those pupils constricted to the bright lights on the ceilings of the train. The carriage started to move sedately so I instincrively sat down and grabbed a book from my bag. It was a hardbound diary, Tuscan inspired covered which I bought at the street market in Perugia. It's a diary, a special book that has been ever my companion especially to start a day and end. I started flicking through the pages and put a cheeky smile on my face as I read the last page where I wrote last:

Nice, October 2008

Bonjour mes amis! I am so very French today sitting here at the shore of the

Mediterranean. I beg you to sympathise with me as I think, I am the happiest

person at the midst of this part of France! Aside from being with Nasser, I saw a lovely woman standing at the waterline on the beach. She was all dressed in white linen, swaying with the strong breeze from the sea. I thought I would like to compose a little poem about her as she gazed far across the ocean as if waiting for a ship to dock or just maybe the sunset, as we all do?

She is the mother I longed to see! The woman whom my life is in debted for and the person I do not want to miss this time!

"Calm down, Leandro! Relax like the way when you were that young, silly boy trying to catch an idwana from an olive tree at your backyard in Sana'a!"

I was watching that woman and deep insid,e I felt how much I missed her! I want to run and hold her and never let her go again yet the right time has never arrived nor ripened just as yet, from that moment on!

I must see you later then,

Leandro

"Paris, Gare du Nord!" a recorded voice woke me up and I felt the train has halted. I have arrived in Paris! I opened my eyes gently and realised that I fell asleep during the entire journey from London to Paris!. The diary was laid on my chest, so I swiftly put it back in the bag and looked around to check that nothing has been missing in any of my valuables. I stood up and carried the bag and left the food and drink that I haven't finished as they have gone cold.

It wass nearly midnight in Paris and the train station was still buzzing with people trying to catch the last train to their final destination-home! I gazed at the timetable and focused on the last train traveling to Nice and whispered to myself, "That will be my final destination!"

I ran to the nearest ticket machine and bought a window seat on the economy class of the SNCF. The train was departing at 2355h and so I sprinted like a headless chicken and boarded into the carriage breathlessly!

"Oh dear! Phew!" I was chasing my breath and looked around and observed the rest of the passengers seated very calmly and seemingly tired after a long day's work. I found my seat but there was a gentleman comfortably sitting who will be right next to me at the end. He was blocking the way with his legs rightly stretched forward. "*Excusez-moi!*" I tried speaking in French in a bastardised accent. The man looked at me and seriously replied, " Yes you may", then immediately followed it with a sarcastic smile.

He stood up and I noticed that he has a bit of a height, about six feet tall.

"*Merci beaucop monsieur!*" I exclaimed and put my bag on the table, then, jumped into the seat and looked outside of the window. It was dark and barely no clouds from above, though, the temperature was less chilly as it was in London. The train began to crawl slowly. I took my huge Bose headphones out from the side pocket of my bag , connected it to my phone and shuffled the tracks played from the music library. I looked at him again before attempting to wear the headphones. He must be on his forties and not sure really if he was French or maybe English. I must have known by now, after all those men that I have gone out with? He was quite good looking with his blue shirt and loosened red necktie.

He must have worked all day as he looked a bit fed up and maybe not interested for a decent conversation throughout our journey? I smiled and as I noticed him stealing looks at me.

“It must have been a very long day for you? “ The gentleman sat up straight and stared at me with his sleepy, blue eyes.

“I am just really glad it is all been such a quite relief, for now!” I answered with a deep sigh then he took a deep breath again himself.

“Where are you heading to?” The stranger asked as he looked very interested to my reply.

“Nowhere! Maybe in the south but I will have to find out in the morning.” I answered in a discreet tone and looked at the window again as the dark views brushed through my tired, green eyes. It was a very early morning and the rest of Europe was still asleep, yet some of us were still on that train waiting to be dragged to our final destination.

“I’m sorry and I didn’t mean anything, but you have a pleasant evening.” A loud voice suddenly roused me again as I was tempted to drift.

“Oh no, it’s absolutely fine! And you too. It really was a long day and I think I am about to start another one again, soon!”

“I am Lean, Leandro!” I whispered but still in a loud voice as all the passengers on the train may have fallen asleep and all they can hear was the friction from the steel on the railway tracks as the iron wheels glided through.

“Loic here!”

I exclaimed as he offered a left handshake. I offered my right hand to accept it and saw a gold band but on the middle finger.

“I actually came from London today and I am just off to the south for a short break.”

I straightened myself but still with both legs on top of the empty seat on the opposite row. I felt more awake then as both of us started some conversations or maybe more? I had to stop my opera music playing as they came out very loud from my headphone speakers. I ended up having the headphones worn just around my neck and not listened to the tracks properly at all.

“You must be French then!” I said in a low voice.

“Yes I am indeed but I studied in London and worked there for a bit so it helped my english a lot!”

Loic replied and began to move himself towards me like we’re almost facing each other.

“I studied at the London School of Economics but that was ages ago and worked at the Blom Bank France. Roughly, I spent three years in England.”

Loic sounded seriously as he scratched his head and stroked his dark grey hair. “How about you? What are you upto?”

The French guy asked with a cheeky grin and raised right eyebrow. I paused and stared outside the flashing views again and felt some exhaustion after those long hours of journey. Someone was making some decent conversation and so must I participate. Maybe at that time I could’ve still maintained to be eloquent and a bit interesting even for just being a co-passenger. Actually, I didn’t even had a clue where our conversation was leading to. I crossed my legs and took a deep breath.

“I just flicked on a very cheap Eurostar ticket today and thought I’ll go to Paris.”

“I have been in school and work all week so I have been really busy. Blom Bank is in Knightsbridge,right? I heard, it’s a distinguished and exclusive bank not just for Parisians in London but also for the residents of Chelsea! I must think I could’ve seen you there? I actually live around that area!”

What a small world!

The calmness of the night sweeped through but broken down by the train steel wheels rolling along the rail tracks. I didn’t notice myself fallen asleep again and just drifted away from that late night conversation. Loic observed me and became very silent whilst carefully looking at my firm chest rising up and down slowly. I slept like a log.

"How boring must I be?" He whispered to himself as he slowly moved and prepared himself to get off the train.

I sensed that guy must be someone very interesting and somebody I must know? I don't know why. I have only met him a couple of hours ago during that time.

I slouched myself on the couch feeling so undisturbed and abandoned by the world. A voice from afar was calling me.

"Lean, my little sweetheart, come to mama!"

A young woman with a long thin black hair was standing outside of a door with open arms enticing a little boy to run and embrace her. He looked so innocent with those long curly hair and olive skin and huge green eyes. he stood up forcibly and walked imperfectly with those soft legs towards her with a silly smile! She embraced him very tight as if they haven't seen each other for a lifetime. She was laughing enormously as she fills him with loads of kisses on his chubby face. She was bursting with tears as they pervade the little boy's face.

"I love you so much, son! My only treasure and the person I would die for!"

The little boy gazed at her sobbing face innocently and unsuspiciously.

"Promise that I will never leave you and will make life better than what I had suffered. You may not be proud of your ancestors but you will build a life that we will all look up and embrace from the heavens above!"

The little boy had no idea what she was whispering about?

Nonetheless, I cannot forget beautiful face of my mother even with so much tears smothered in her bright, brown eyes. Those words had kept me going all through these years and have always haunted me to be the best person she ought me to become. I'm sure every mother would want the best for their children but some are just too fortunate to become someone without even knowing it? Not sublime but no hard work to put on, yet, amazing how they get there into the end?

The SNCF halted into a full stop and that roused me but not entirely as I sedately opened my teary eyes. I have reached Nice but it isn't my final destination yet. I started recollecting the events that happened along the entire journey and all I could remember was that French guy who's gentle and interesting? I wasn't sure? I thought that was really rude of me falling asleep in the middle of a decent conversation but you never know? He could've been a bloody thief just pretending and then I made sure I had everything on me intact! He must have abused me whilst I was sleeping and why did I not feel anything then? God, I can't be so pathetic after being with all those men in my very young age?

"I think I have everything on my bag, phone and notebook."

I noticed my linen shirt looked enormously crumpled and with an odour of sweet sweat altogether with the Acqua di Parma that I wore since yesterday morning. I badly needed a shower or maybe a dip into the Mediterranean sea. I've got everything in my hands and maybe I do not need to wear the jacket? I felt the warm breeze of southern France and still it was summer even at the end of the season. I stepped out of the train and took a deep breath. What a gaze of an utterly different life? The station was quite busy on a Wednesday morning. I rotated a Cartier watch on my right wrist to confirm the time and it said, 0615h.

"That is not true? I told myself and tried to feel the phone on my right jacket pocket. I believed the phone will self adjust the time and it must be seven-ish. Along with the phone, there was a little paper and I didn't have any idea what it was. I looked at it and it was a business card so I began reading it with so much curiousity? My left eyebrow raised as I read:

"Loic De Coteau, International Cooperation Manager of BNP Parribas! Hmmm...it has his work and mobile number and so has his email address too?" I looked up with a cheeky grin.

The night lights of the train station were still on and looked really bright. I felt the rays of the sunlight coming through the glazed, painted glasses penetrating intensely.

"Damn, he must be something else I should take into consideration?" I asked myself and a thought crossed my mind.

"Maybe I will call him just to apologise how disrespectful I was? I thought it was a boorish display, wasn't it?"

I was still standing next to the platform with all those thoughts distracting me and decided to give him an early morning call. I dialed his mobile number written on the card and I can hear a humming noise. It usually is when your phone is brought abroad and switched to a roaming mode.

"Bonjour!" Loic answered with a sleepy voice.

"Hey it's me, Lean! I am sorry to wake you up but I wanted to sincerely apologise for what happened last night."

"I must be really tired?" I talked fast and straight without even asking if it was really him.

"Ahahaha, it's ok and I understand 'cos you looked really tired and I can imagine myself. I would do the same?" His voice became more loud and awake.

"I am sorry Loic and I wish to catch up with you again, soon?" I replied with so a hint of invitation but that was me as you may have known by now?

"No, don't worry at all and you let me know. Where are you now, anyway?"

"I mean, you have a great time whatever you are doing in France, Lean!"

He sounded more intertwined but I knew I have so many other concerns for the day. Mister Frenchman will have to be put aside for that time being. It doesn't sound so me-not a very Lean sort of statement at all. When did you think I would ever refuse a man, nor who has ever let go of me from their radar?

"Sorry Loic, I have to go! But I really appreciate the fact that we met! I will get in touch with you, I promise."

"I am just really here for a very personal reason. I'll see you later, ciao!" I wanted to talk to him more but I realised that would cost me a lot too with all the roaming charges so I guessed there will be some other ways especially when I get back to England.

I walked out of the station swiftly and was sure and definite that the Europecar Rental was just two blocks away. I reserved a small car which was a promo for two days and half the price. The station was filled with lots of tourists, mostly older adults. The region was known for its genuine history from the land and to the sea. It was where everyone would spend the rest of their summer as the warm weather was still non par to any European destinations. I smelled the fresh breads and coffee but I have to stop myself for messing about, after all, I wasn"t in London I believed.

I noticed that the French in the southern region are so laid back and life seemed to be on the opposite side of New York or London. It's true! So I took my time and trotted along the pavements until I reached the car rental shop.

That was very quick! It was an eastern European lady on the counter, maybe Polish with her funny English-French accent. She was so friendly and nearly gave the car free of charge. But of course, she can't afford to lose her job that time of the day?

I drove a silver Peugot 206, quite brand new and automatic. What a lovely scenery driving along Cote D'Azur. Along the road, there were plenty of cyclists, joggers and rollerbladers. In London, yes, all these cyclists owned the road and seemed worst in France. I felt more awake now having been driving along the coast of the Promenade des Anglais. What a breath of fresh air coming to the Mediterranean Sea with the gorgeous turquoise body of water brushing through the white pebbled shore. It was just fascinating! Why can't life be like that forever? To have forgetten about school and not thinking of going back to Yemen?

My heart rate started to rise more rapidly as I drove along the highways on the cliffs of the French Riviera. I felt a mixed of emotions but I should've been excited and not anxious in meeting a very special person again. That was the moment I longed for many years. 'Twas an opportunity for us to reunite and start all over again as a family. Instead, I looked at the gilded mansions and some dubious architectures displayed, overhanging the stunning mountains as a diversion. The dark blue sky from above was just highlighted by the ray of sunshine so close to the sea.

I have reached Menton, a small town just before Monaco. It's quite Italianated with all the café restaurants scattered all over the town. Its surroundings were less ostentatious than Monte Carlo, though they're close. I passed through the old townhall and some mosaic architectures may need some refurbishments but they represented the historical town in such a distinctive way.

I was driving uphill and the road was coarse and bumpy. The place seemed like a huge botanical garden with plenty of lemon trees. I was approaching a tall, Italian inspired house in yellow and white. The lemon trees were lined to guide a narrow path through the building with a variety of green bushes around; thick and needed trimming I would say. The house was a bit old fashioned but looked like a holiday home for retired couples and the atmosphere suggested a very unwinding environment.

Chapter Twenty Two

I stepped out of the car and left it parked in front of the main door. I stood just in the middle of the building and gazed on it from the ground to the roof. It was a tall villa. The antique door looked very old as the red wood peeled in tiny fibres. The gothic carvings were still noticeable but was crying out loud for a delicate varnish soon. A horse shoe metal was hanged to knock and it was quite difficult. It seemed to have not been used regularly and needed some oil or grease. I managed to knock twice and heard someone's tiny footsteps increasingly loud towards me on the other side of the wooden entrance.

"*Oui*?" A woman's voice slipped through with hesitation.

"*Bonjour madame*! *Je suis venu pour voir,* Suhaila?" I answered with my poor French. I wished I could be more fluent than that. I only learned the basic ones in my French class ages ago. I wished it was right though?

She opened the door and was shocked to see me. She knew who I was!

"Lean, *ana habibti!"* She yelled and wrapped her arms around me. She bursted into tears and I felt them damping my right shoulder.

"Mama, *inti whashtini*! Where have you been all these years?"

"I have been searching and waiting for you but you disappeared!"

"How come you're here, Mama?" My voice shivered and my eyes soaked in tears. I didn't feel hating her as I missed her so much! I thought of so many questions but didn't know what to ask first.

"*Alhamdulillah, alhamdulillah!*" He heard all my prayers as I asked of you every night and day. This is the day that He made for us to be reunited again!"

She looked at me in the eyes and held my shoulders firmly. She has not changed much, although, I noticed some fine lines on her forehead and the sides of her eyes. Her hair was still long and black but I could spot some few white streaks.

"*Alhamdulillah,* Mama!" I have waited so long for this too and I prayed so hard every night!" I continued sobbing and trembling deep inside.

"Where is baba? Is he here too, Mama?" I asked with a crying voice.

"Come inside!"

It's such a very long story my son. But I will tell you so be strong as you have been all these years." She sounded as if she knew everything about me as I have been away from her for so many years.

She brought me inside the house and laid my bag on a brown, fabric sofa. The place looked amazing with an old plaster fireplace. The floor was marbled with black and white and the ceiling with wood and white cement. A huge flat TV was hanged on the wall and I saw a stack of DVDs and a cabinet of books in the living area. I felt like I was at home in Sana'a and not in Menton, France.

"Are you hungry, my son?" Mama asked and I traced her voice coming from a very modern kitchen.

She still loved being in the kitchen and experimenting with food. It was a mix of all black and white ceramics and granite. The cupboards were all white painted and everything must have been kept behind all those cabinets. Mama was so organised in the kitchen, although, too messy everytime she cooks but her aftercare was fantastic. She learned it from her parents in Malaysia. They said it is a reflection of how people are in the house. Mama have always used her past experiences in her daily life and believed what her parents taught her were essential things in life.

"I cooked some roast chicken in lemon and fresh garden leaves salad. You must be hungry, *habibi*!" She yelled and I saw her walking about in the kitchen.

She hasn't answered my question yet about my father and what strength should I need when she told me to be prepared for? She walked passed me and went through a backdoor with a plate of a whole roasted chicken in her hands. She wore a white apron and thick gloves and looked like a chef. I followed her and saw a garden at the backyard. It was astonishing! A good piece of land surrounded by lemon trees at their peak of bearing fruits. The green leaves and yellow fruits complemented each other with the blue skies on the background. The floor was cobbled with limestones. It was a little paradise hidden at the back of an old house. She placed the food on a wooden table and invited me to sit down.

"You must be very tired, *habibi*!" She exclaimed.

"I'll be back in a sec. Make yourself comfortable, ok?"

I sat down and felt the warmth of sunshine. The wooden chair has warmed my bottom too and my back. The chicken smelled so delicious and I felt my tummy gagging for it. Mama came back with plates and cutleries. On her other hand, she was holding a glass pitcher of a frozen lemonade. I saw some sliced lemons mixed with ice. It looked so refreshing!

"*Buona petit!*"

"When did you learn French, Mama? You sound so amazing!"

"It's still not very good, son."

"I rarely go out and meet people so I still need to make some more improvements." She smiled whilst arranging the dishes on the table. She sat right in front of me and changed the look on her face. My mother looked up at the skies and closed her eyes.

"*Alhamdullilah!* For this wonderful day and these delicious foods. Also, for bringing my son home safely." She prayed.

The chicken was so warm and tender. My eyes were closed on each and every bite. She still cooked the same and delicious as ever. The sweet potatoes were so rich and creamed in my mouth. I was speechless for a while, savouring my Mama's speciality. She poured a glassful of lemonade and prepared it for me. It was so cool and refreshing-bitter but really sweet at the end. Surely I wanted to eat and drink more!

"Lean, your baba was gone a longtime ago."

"He put and end to his life and so he's in the heavens with *Allah*."

"I am so sorry, son." She spoke in a low and calm voice. She looked down but didn't look sad.

I paused and laid the knife and fork on the plate. I thought I was going to leap for joy and celebrate. The man that I hated most has paid for all his trespasses. He deserved it and therefore should face *Allah* with plenty of regrets! But he is still my father as his blood runs through my veins. I still owe my life to him and he's one of the reasons of my existence.

"I am so sorry, Lean!" Mama held my hands so and squeezed them. She came near and hugged me. I didn't realise I was in tears until she began kissing my eyes and cheeks. I felt the dampness of her lips against my skin, yet, she remained silent and composed.

"Mama, I do not know if I want to rejoice or weep."

"Baba has given you so much pain and all these years of being away from you."

"My heart breaks with all your miseries in his midst."

"Shhh…it's over now. It's all over now, son."

"*Alhamdullilah*! He has been good to us. We have moved on to a sweet life at the end!"

"Look at you now, you have grown and matured enormously! I was never wrong with Mr. Al Sadeq. He looked after you so well!"

"Of course and the IS too!"

"Mama, how did baba die?" I asked as I helped myself wiping all those tears.

"Why did he kill himself? I didn't want him to go that way."

"I have been thinking about him all these years and I have missed him. He visits me in my dreams, Mama."

Seemed like we have forgotten about our food and Mama hasn't eaten anything. The chicken has gone cold now and the ice chips have turned into water inside the pitcher. The afternoon felt warmer but the lemon trees gave shade and protected us from the scorching heat of the sun. She poured me more of the juice and led me to lie down on a chair bed underneath a lemon tree. We left the food and the dishes on the table. I laid down with my head on her lap. I felt drifted apart from reality and hoped my Mama would tell me more about the years that made us distant and away from each other.

I looked up at my mother's beautiful face. Her bright, brown eyes and smooth skin haven't changed that much. The clear blue sky was so bright and clear on her background. She began stroking my fine hair and gazed at me like she doesn't want to miss anything as she looked at me closely. She seemed like observing me closely and taking notes of every detail of my looks.

"Your baba and I loves you so much!"

H"e would always ask about you and how you were doing in school everytime he comes home from his flights."

"One day, I came home from the *suk* and found the whole house flooded with water. The bathroom pipes leaked and there was water all over the house. At first, I tried to fix it but I needed an expert to do it at the end. I called your Uncle Tareq and so he came. He was able to fix it right away and I started cleaning up all the mess. He helped me and it took us all afternoon to dry all the carpets. Tareq had himself wet and soiled. He borrowed your father's clothes and their sizes were quite the same." She sighed and took another deep breath at the end.

"Knowingly, your father arrived that evening and he was drunk. Tareq stayed for dinner as he wanted to see your father too. We were so surprised as it never occurred to your father. He was so distressed and we asked him what was wrong?"

"He asked me what your uncle was doing at our house at that time of the night and he became so furious about it. I tried to explain the situation but he never gave me a chance. He grabbed me and asked, since when

I have been seeing your uncle? I was astounded by his acts. He was swearing and shouting so loud."

"Tareq stopped him and they ended up with a brawl. They both wrestled in the living area and most of the glasswares shattered into pieces. Your uncle didn't fight back but tried to stop your father from being so agitated and aggressive. I tried to stop your father too but he hit me and your uncle saw it. He threatened Tareq with a gun and sent him away. We were so terrified by him and had no power to overrule his dominance."

Mama started to cry as she narrated all what happened in the past. I felt really guilty as I haven't had the chance to defend her and stayed by her against my father's oppression. She was looking from afar with her watery eyes and never blinked.

"You have to know something, Lean. I beg for your forgiveness as I have kept this for so long."

"You're a grown up now and this time, no one can ever take you away from me."

"You're father lost his inheritance when he married me and that was the price he paid because he loved me so much. I truly honor and respect him for choosing me more than the wealth he can have in this world. He said his job will sustain us and I believed him. I didn't grow in wealth nor power so I could live a simple life and he promised that we will do it together."

"His brother had all their family's possession at the end and they made sure that your baba will suffer and come back home begging for food and remorse."

"Jawad was sacked from work and didn't know where to go as any other airline refused to hire him."

"One day, he came home and told me that he lost his job and will try to find another one. But fate was absolutely appalling until we had nothing to eat and nowhere to live."

"Tareq came to visit us one day and was so wretched. He apologised for their parents' deeds and there we knew, they suppressed all the opportunities that your father had so we have nowhere to go."

"Your Baba was massively furious but couldn't do anything. He was powerless and weak…can't pick up the pieces. Very frustrated!"

"Your uncle had an indecent proposal and we were extremely disgusted!"

"I would have to sleep with him for one night and he will give half of his affluences to your father."

Mama paused and stopped crying. I was shocked and now I just don't loathe my father but also his brother. Uncle Tareq who was like a second father to me has unbelievably thought of such an intention? He was like those other men who were known to me too…bastard!

"You father didn't have any second thoughts and he'd rather crawl in mud to provide me food and shelter. I offered him to come home with me to Malaysia but there was no certainty of good life there. I haven't been in touch with my family and my father would refuse to take me back again, I swore. He was a man of pride and resentment."

"We slept for many nights in cold and hunger. We were evicted from the apartment as your father ran out of money from his savings. His friends turned us down and one night, we were the only two people in the dark streets of Sana'a. There was hail and strong winds. Your father was cold and coughing until blood came out from his mouth. I was so terrified and didn't know what to do. We knocked on people's houses and everyone refused to let us in. We found a barn and we warmed ourselves in a haystack with the animals. Jawad was still coughing with blood and he was burning with high fevers."

"I fed him with milk that I squeezed out from the goats surrounded us. I was so good with animals back I when I was farming in Malaysia."

Her story was incredibly shocking! I closed my eyes in tears. I didn't seem to believe what she was telling me. Mama sounded so sincere and looked like she has more to tell.

"I was crying silently and only thought of one answer to every suffering we were going through that night."

"Jawad fell asleep with his body half-covered with dry weeds. He laid on a log and looked like he was dying to have that rest for ages."

"I kissed his cold lips and whispered words of forgiveness and bid him goodbye."

"I left him peacefully and walked away. I never turned my back to see him again. My heart was breaking and crying but promised that life would never be that miserable again for him."

"I went straight into your uncle Tareq's house and knocked at his door on that early dawn. He looked half-asleep as he opened the door and found me with my old clothes dripping from the pouring rain. I fell in his arms and lost the will to live. I was starved for so many days and my energy has ceased to keep me going."

"I woke up in a comfy bed. The atmosphere was filled with a breath of fresh air but my head felt so heavy that time. It was midday when I glanced at the clock. I tried to remember where I was and I definitely knew where. I forced myself to get up and found out I was naked underneath a white blanket. I cried with so much tears and cursed that day!"

"That time, the world can turn me down and your father can curse or kill me. I paid the price for him to have his life back and I was ready to die! I have nothing left for myself! No pride, no honour, no dignity, no more! I could be stoned until I gasp for the last breath and die!" She was sobbing and wobbling in tears.

I remained speechless. I could hate her for betraying my father but it's too late now. It happened many years ago. She sacrificed her life to have gone this far for me and to everyone else in our family.

"I saw Tareq coming out of the shower just covered with a black towel wrapped around his waist. He smiled mischievously and told me not to worry as he had been so gentle all throughout the night. I refused to look at him and felt so sick and ill. He came near me and promised to give us everything we needed. He asked for more of my femininity and I wasn't able to refuse in as much as I wanted to."

"Forgive me, my son. I am so sorry as I wasn't genuine and pure. You may go away and leave me in disgrace! I am very sinful!"

She looked at the skies and her tears fell on me. My heart was breaking and crushing too. I sympathised with her and agonised of what she has gone through. She was in so much pain! She doesn't deserve it!

"Your father was brought into the military hospital and he suffered from severe pneumonia. He recovered hastily as I helped with all his care. I lived at the hospital accommodation all throughout and took nearly three months for him to recuperate. He asked how did he manage to live and I told him that the Yemenia Airlines provided some insurances for his healthcare. He was promised a better job when he gets back into his feet and that encouraged him to get better swiftly. They said, he was an asset to the company and wanted him back."

Tareq has never reappeared and left us in peace. He promised with his words and everytime I face your father, my heart was squashed and my mind filled with so much guilt. He thanked *Allah* and reminded me that the heavens will never forsake us no matter what happens."

"Jawad eventually acquired his high position again at the same airline company and was more sensible with money and loving the job and the company so much more. He was the most successful and trained so many Yemenis to study aeronautics. I became pregnant and that was you, *ana habibi*!" She smiled with a drop of tear from her left eye. She wiped her face and sighed. Her story must have ended now, happily!

"You were the joy of our lives. Your Baba comes home frequently and flies less as his job was more land-based. The extra flights were paid on top of his job and so we managed to buy the piece of land where our house in Sana'a was built."

"One day, your father came home and surprised me with an unexpected guest. It was your uncle Tareq. He said, they bumped into each other in a flight. Your uncle begged your father for pardon and for many years, they have forgotten all about it. I was very anxious that Tareq would tell your father about what happened when I left him in the barn but there was no conversation about it during that evening. They reconciled and became really closed brothers again like they were during their childhood. Tareq never said anything to me but treated me as his brother's wife with so much respect. I thought he was only showing it because we're in front of his brother but he made me realised that he has transformed into a better person and the past should never be dwelt for as life moves on."

"Your father and uncle became business partners and they put up an engineering and construction company. They started building houses and hired more architects and engineers. Your *baba* borrowed money from the bank but he eventually paid them off as their business had grown successfully. They became huge in Sana'a and started constructing buildings and contracted other known companies abroad. Jawad still loved Yemenia and remained with the airline even if he didn't need to. He aimed to prove his family wrong and that wealth can be earned with patience and hard work. He was right!"

"You grew so fast and we adored you more and more. We planned your future especially your education that I have never had. We wanted you to study in a foreign school and be productive to the society. That was why I have been reading so many english writings when you were little. Your father wanted some more children as you were five years of age and we still haven't managed to have more. We have eventually moved to our new house in *Al Hatarish.* It was a dream come true and a new home for us. Little did I know, that house was the root of all the bitterness and sorrows of our lives." Her voice became louder and I rose myself from her lap. I didn't understand what she meant.

"What do you mean, mama?" I looked at her in the eyes and saw her gazed on the lemon trees surrounding us.

"We went to see a specialist to help us bear another child as we were both so worried. We were quite young still and seemed that there was something wrong, why can't we not have another child. The doctor revealed that your father has been completely sterile due to high radiation exposure from his job. He was shocked and I felt really sorry for him. He cried and never spoken to me until we reached home that day."

"There he knew and gave me doubts of my infidelity. He was fuming in anger and laid his hands on me until I bled and begged him to stop. I kneeled in front of him and kissed his feet and wrapped them all with my tears. He kicked me away and felt so ill being his wife. He wanted me to go away and never come back. He wanted me to die and suffer in pain like the way he felt when he was sick, hungry and cold. His self-respect as a man has gone and his dignity was lost because of me. I took them all away and I was willing to fulfill his wishes if it would have given his self-esteem back."

"He strangled me and asked, who was responsible for you. Without any further ado, I brought him back to the times when we were in the cold streets and in the midst of the animals in the barn. He was fast asleep when I left him and agreed to an indecent proposal!"

"If his nobility was lost, then how about my dignity as a woman?"

"I begged for a moment to explain myself but he was seething and holding his head like not knowing what to do next."

"If I hadn't done it, then both of us were found cold and rotten dead! Him, especially!"

It was a real shocker, knowing my real father was uncle Tareq? The man how I longed to be my real father came true during those moments. My heart leapt in so much joy and the skies became brighter as I looked the way up above. I embraced my mama so tightly and I was howling in tears. She never knew my exultance about the truth of who my real father was.

"Where is my uncle Tareq, mama?"

"Have you ever seen him again? At all?"

I stood up and pottered around the garden. I couldn't believe all those events happened in many years and may probably have just in that entire afternoon. I was excited, anxious and stirred! I was completely and utterly roused by her story about my uncle Tarcq.

Chapter Twenty Three

"Your father is in France! Your uncle Tareq is here!"

"He owns this house and he will be arriving at dinner time!" She exclaimed.

"He bought this house for us and we have lived here peacefully and happily."

"Tareq is a Corporate Engineer of the *Electricite de France* here in the southern region. I'm sure you've heard about the EDF, Lean?"

"When your baba died, his family took his body away and I was never welcomed to see him. They severely despised me and held me responsible for his death and misfortune. I had nowhere to go but home, in Malaysia where my own family was. I received all of his shares and pensions and they were more than enough for me to get out of Yemen and disappear silently."

"I went home with hopes that my parents would welcome me back and forgive me after all those years. Unfortunately, my parents died not long after I have left. My eldest sister was my only family left and hardly recognised her. Sanisah looked old in her age and I found out that she suffered from breast cancer for many years. She didn't marry at all and lived by herself in our small hut and remained to be a farmer. Her situation was dreadful and it didn't surprise me. I brought her to Kuala Lumpur for treatment but the cancer has spread in her lungs and bones. The doctors did everything as I offered all the money that I have but she died after a few weeks. Sanisah was very pleased to see me and I made sure she was comfortable and didn't have any pain until her last breath. I was on her side all throughout her last days. I buried her next to my parents and prayed that we will all see each other soon in heaven!"

"I rang Tareq in Sana'a and told him that I was in Malaysia. I had no family left even with the plenty of wealth that I brought back home. It would never take them back to life again. Tareq found a business partner in the south of France and traveled more in Europe."

"One day, he surprisingly appeared in front of my apartment in Kuala Lumpur. I cannot forget that day. He looked so different wearing a coat and tie. All shaven and I hardly recognised him as I used to see him wearing a *tob.* He attended a conference in Singapore and Kuala Lumpur. He stayed in KL for a week and we met for dinner every night during his entire stay. Every night was special and we talked so much of our past and those memories. He was a different man and I must admit, I began to like him more and more than Jawad. I have forgiven him and his sincerity has won my heart!"

"We never wasted any time and believed, we were all matured individuals who could start a better life and rebuild a family again. We talked so much about you and thought of you. One day, we will live together as a happy family again. *Inshallah!*"

"Tareq loved France as it's a beautiful place where he thought we could be all away from anyone who knew and recognised us. He easily got a job at EDF with a massive help from Mr. Al Sadeq. May his soul rest in peace. His death was so sudden and unbelievable!"

"We were so shocked when we heard about his death, son!"

"When Tareq knew all about you as his child, he was in a daze! He didn't know what to do. I only told him when he came to see me in Malaysia. Your *baba* and I kept it for many years. Jawad felt so ashamed of himself and I sympathised with him. We were sure that if the family knew all about it, Tareq would lose all his rights too but he didn't care."

"Tareq hated me for hiding the truth about you. He never thought of me lying after all these years. I did it for a very good purpose, although it was still something that he should have known a long time ago. He understood that it may not have changed our relationships together and the right time came for him to know all about it and for you as well."

"I am so sorry, son. Forgive me, *habibi.*"

Mama looked at me and held my hands. We went and sat near the cliff, on the rocks overlooking a beautiful blue sea. It was calm and surreal. The warmth of the air has lessened and as we looked back, we saw our beautiful house covered with lemon trees at the back.

"I can't wait to see uncle Tareq, mama. I don't know what to call him, maybe papa?" I glanced at her and smiled with my lips sealed. She only looked at me and gazed at the views at the front again.

"You can call him whatever you want, son. I'm sure he wouldn't mind. He is always looking forward to see you and call you son. He is a very nice man as you may have known."

"I pray that there will be less lemons in our lives as we start anew."

"*Alhamdullilah* to the ever rich soil in Menton."

"I have grown so many lemons after all these years and it never failed me to harvest plenty!"

"Lemons, mama? I don't understand?" I asked her with my right brow raised.

"What are you talking about? What's with the lemons in our lives?"

"When I was little, my mother told me a tale about a young couple who lived in a small village in Sabah, on the coast. The woman's husband was a fisherman and he always comes home with a really foul stink from all his catches. When he arrives home from fishing, his wife fills up a tank of rain water to bathe her husband and get rid of the stench. The old man always moaned about it and told her wife about their miserable life and wished he could do more better than fishing. The woman prayed hard one night when there was hard rain and thunderstorms. She asked the gods of how can she be more useful to her partner and wished to suffer for him in the name of love. The poor man came home without a single catch and his wife was nowhere to be found? He fell asleep whilst waiting for his wife in their little terrace and in the morning when he woke up, he found a huge tank in front of their hut filled with fresh creatures from the sea without a single stink. A short tree has grown right next to it with green leaves and yellow, round fruits. He never recognised the plant and never saw it before. The man cried out loud and looked at the clouds above. As his tears fall into the soil, the fruits multiplied and covered the whole tree.

"My dear wife!" He shouted.

"I will weep and complain no more!"

"You never deserved to bear the fruits of my sorrows!"

"Then, he fell into the ground and took his last breath so he can never moan again!"

"Sorry son, you always knew how boring I am with all my funny stories since you were little."

"Never mind!"

"No, mama. I miss and always longed for your stories."

"I love listening to them."

"I will tell them to others, too! You don't mind, do you, mama?"

"No, not at all son!"

Chapter Twenty Four

Dear Mr. Fitzgerald,

Bonjour!

I woke up today and realised I haven't slept like I did for so many nights before.

I used to have so many nightmares and dreamt of dreams that disturbed me even they were a reminiscence of my past. Yet, they say every night is a different story as the curtains close and the show ends.

You must have waited for bloody ages and now my story is all set for you. Maybe not as planned but as we agreed.

Here's a story of my true experience of life, love and finding true happiness. It actually is an occurrence of a lifetime and doesn't stop just for now…

"Maybe I'll leave that on my diary for now and give him a call later!"

The banging of the window roused me gently. I forcibly opened my eyes and the sun beam strucked me placidly. I wasn't hurt! The beige linen curtains sway gently along the glass door. I felt the subtle warmth of fresh air embraced me.

I figured it out! I am in another place as I was blown by a tender breeze coming from the Mediterranean sea. The evening was so surreal but the seagulls squeal break the stillness of sunset.

It's the last few days of summer in the south of France. I found myself laid on a wooden chairbed in the middle of the garden. I fell asleep after that very long day and night of journey and reunion with my Mama.

She left me in peace and that was vey rude of me again. Her stories moved me and I'm sure there was more to tell.

The surrounding atmosphere was covered with an orangy hue as the sun was setting in. I dragged myself up and decided to get back into the house and searched for my mother. She was sitting at the kitchen table whilst having tea with a man- my real father!

"Uncle Tareq!" I exclaimed as my whole body froze and undecided what to do. I really missed him though. I grew up with him around and treated me like a son. And now, thinking that he is my real father!

"Lean, son? I'm your papa now!" He answered in an endearing voice.

I ran towards him and embraced him. He hasn't changed after all these long years. He was still taller than me but I noticed some grey streaks on his hair- they became thinner now. His beard was still grown black and thick, quite simile when we were still in Sana'a. He hugged me and moved me closer to him. I can smell a faint perfume dispersed in all his sweat. He has been out all day in the field for his engineering works presumably. He actually looked very European now with his shirt and trousers unlike before, he loved wearing his white *tob* and leather sandals. Mama came and held us both. It was the happiest moment of my life being with my parents again-especially with my real father whom I have always wished to be!

"Mama, sorry!"

"I fell asleep this afternoon but don't worry, I have almost every story that you told me, promise."

"I know, you were very tired, son. But we have more plenty of time, so don't worry." She replied in tears as she wiped my face and gazed at me tenderly.

"I have always prayed for this day and *Allah* has been always on our side."

"Thank You so much!" Mama was sobbing with tears and I felt them damping my ear. She was shaking and very emotional that time. Papa was quite still but I felt him trembling inside.

Mama cooked a wonderful supper that night. We had roast lamb, cucumber and olive salad with plenty of feta cheese. Baba roasted some red potatoes and brought truffles and custard flans too. Mama has still managed to make those freshly squeezed lemonade very refreshing! I still couldn't believe that my old uncle Tareq was my real father since then? I prayed to *Allah* that my baba should be happy for us and may he rest in His bosom peacefully.

That lovely night, Papa and I stayed up so late playing chess and didn't stop until he defeated me at the end. I was way off playing better now and thanks to the old master Juergen. Sometimes, I can still remember him every now and again. I thought he was my first love as he helped me know myself for who I was really and proud for who I am. Long years have gone passed now and here I am reminiscing all the bitterness of my past.

Mama stayed late too in the kitchen perfecting her lemon marmalade. I can't wait to have them on my croissants for breakfast in the morning! She must have cropped a bountiful of lemons from her garden. No wonder she reaped all the goodness of the bitter fruit with sweetness at the end. Her myth was indeed a fact and maybe I should grow lemons too. But Mama has grown them all for us! Blessed are her lemon trees; for them, they bear fruits that carry the graves of our past!

Chapter Twenty Five

My eyes slowly opened and gazed outside the half- opened window. I can imagine a glare of sunshine if I open it wide. I prayed that a strong wind would detour or else I might melt like a vampire if the sun striked me at that time in the morning. The Italian inspired wooden window opened outward a bit and the white -laced curtain swayed sedately. The seagulls must be streaming along, up and down in the air as I can hear their shrill squeak.

I searched for my watch or maybe my phone will do. At least I could see any missed calls or texts that I have ignored for the last twenty-four hours. What a lovely day, it was indeed! What an eccentric way of spending the last days of summer in Menton, France. Someone must be gearing up and about in the kitchen. I heard the pots and pans striking each other and the smell of freshly baked bread was such a bliss! It must be my Mama. She hasn't changed and I remembered her doing all of these in the years when we were in Sana'a. She would wake up so early and prepare breakfast especially when my baba was on holiday with us. She looked after us so well.

I rose up from a huge bed and felt my loose pyjama moving down my waist. Papa Tareq gave this to me last night. I loved the comfort of the thin, blue linen and string, snuggling around my waist.

"Maybe I should go down and help Mama?"

"I could surprise them for an English breakfast? Or that could be a shocker?"

I walked down through the red tiled stairs and followed where the noise was. I saw Mama's back with a yellow apron wrapped around her body.

She was wearing a green, thin dress, still with covered shoulders and clothed down below her knees. Her hair has remained long and black. My Mama was the same lovely woman I have ever known.

"*Saba al ker,* Mama!" I greeted her like we used in arabic.

"Good morning, *habibi*!"

She replied and turned her back to face me. She moved forward and came near me. I embraced her, tightly and I can smell the sweetness of her sweat from her hair. I missed my mother so much after all these years of longing and forlorn. I don't want to let go of her now. Her absence has inspired me to achieve liberty and determination in life.

"Come, my son. Let's bring all these foods outside the garden!"

"The weather is perfect today, unlike in Sana'a, we have it all year round."

She started grabbing the basket of croissants and offered it to me. Then, carried a tray with a pot of coffee, milk and sugar.

"I will come back for the rest, don't worry." She added as she lead the way to the back door.

I saw a plate of different cheeses and olives on the wooden table. She must be referring to those.

"Mama, is papa awake now?" I exclaimed whilst following on her back.

She opened the back door and I can easily view the stunning garden with those thin, grassed floor. On the sides, there grew some olive trees with green fruits on them and still, those lemon trees at the edges. A variety of potted flowers were arranged on the sides and I can't identify any of those. They're just amazing. We headed down to a set of table and chairs made of dark rattan. The sun was up and I felt the warmth of sunshine scorching my back and arms. I realised we were at the edge of a cliff and then I saw the sea from afar.

"This is stunning, Mama!" I yelled as I looked around and gathered all the views.

The blue water from the sea looked so calm and still. The reflection of the sun were just incredibly like silver dusts sowed over a blue mantle. It's a perfect day!

"Good morning all!" Papa cried out as he was standing at the door with the plate of those different cheeses on his grasp.

I ran towards him and kissed his forehead. He tried to hold the plate with his one hand and grabbed my hands and kissed them. We have a great respect for one another. I can see a few lines on his forehead and a few streaks of grey hair. His looks were quite similar to my baba, yet, he is my father now- my real papa!

"Son, go and grab any of my shirt and cover yourself! You are such an English boy now." He added and tapped my shoulder.

I realised, I was at home with an Arab family, though we're in Europe, these people were still the old fashioned and most traditional muslims. I ran inside and went upstairs to their bedroom and searched for a top. Their bedroom was massive with a king sized wooden bed. It was so organised and it must be my Mama's fault. I saw a dark chest drawer and that must be where he kept some of his clothes. On top of the drawer, there were several photo frames with pictures of me from school in Yemen and some from London too! Nasser should be blamed for all of these? How amazing was that man!

"Lean, quickly my dear!" Mama yelled as I heard her voice coming from the kitchen.

I grabbed a loose white t-shirt from the drawer and quickly put it on. I smelled a man's strong perfume on it and I can't identify what it was. I ran out of the room and passed the other bedroom where I slept that night. My phone was ringing and I thought not to answer it as I would get charged more for those roaming services. I came back and got into the room and looked who could that be and I saw Kevin was trying to ring me. I picked it up but I wanted to let him know where I was! A lovely place in France called heaven!

"Hello, Kevin!"

"I am far away so I will call you on skype later or maybe email you?" I muttered with my eyes continued to explore my new bedroom.

"I understand. I won't be long but just to let you know, I have made a commitment to Devonshire Publishing."

"I have written your story as a book with a great deal!"

"I am still curious though, what ending should it be?"

"I hope you're having a good time and not coming home broken hearted again, my dear?" Kevin exclaimed with great excitement and sympathy.

"That's fantastic, Kevin! I am totally stunned. I cant imagine myself as a character on a book. I mean, a book of myself? I answered and felt limpy and totally zoned out.

"Well, better be quick before they change their minds!"

I'll speak to you soon, Lean!"

"Behave yourself and write a happy ending, ok?" Kevin yelled and put the phone down.

The phone was still on my right ear as I was holding it. Kevin must be joking me but I knew him. He always meant business and he is the man!

"Leandro, it's lunch time soon, son!"

"Time is ticking fast, never waste it."

"Come on!" Papa shouted from the garden.

He was right. I should never waste time and make my story a happy ending after all the hurdles along those unbelievable ways. Nevertheless, it's worth crossing all those barriers. Look at me now, at the finale with the curtains closing soon.

I went down and headed to the garden where my parents were waiting. I was looking at a perfect couple looking after each other as I approach my mama and papa. My mama was serving all the mugs with coffee and papa was arranging all the cutleries. I looked at the sky and it was all clear and blue! I sat down and joined them. We were a family again, bound and strengthened after all those years.

“Are you happy, son?” Mama asked and looked at me with tears gently flowing from her bright, brown eyes.

“Your Mama has ever longed for this to ensue!”

“We are so pleased you’re here, son!” Papa added and held my shoulder.

“I kept longing for this too and thought it will never happen.”

The long time for searching has never been wasted as they were filled with great memories that I won’t regret.

“But I am home now with you- mama, papa.”

I must say, this is such a happy ending!

“I love you both so much!” I replied with a sudden descent of tears from my eyes.

Dear Mr. Fitzgerald,

Bonjour!

I woke up today and realised I haven’t slept like I did for so many nights before.

I used those nightmares and dreamt of dreams that disturbed me even if they were a reminiscence of my past. Yet, they say every night is a different story as the curtains close and the show ends.

You must have waited for bloody ages and now my story is all set for you. Maybe not as planned but as we have agreed.

Here’s a story of my true experience of life, love and finding true happiness. It actually is an occurrence of a lifetime and doesn’t stop just for now.

May your readers be entertained and find the lemons of their bittersweet journey of life. I have found mine through my parents so I got away from planting and nurturing them in my own little garden of life.

You'll never know, somebody out there has started to gather a lemon seed and sowed it to grow too. Others could maybe found underneath a lemon tree sobbing or laughing in tears whilst reading and finishing this book by now.

Merci beaucop monsieur, Kevin!

Yours truly,

Leandro Jawad Al Bahir

Chapter Twenty Six

"Mister Leandro Jawad Al Bahir, *Summa cum- laude*!" A loud, man's voice from the surround speakers covered the entire Royal Albert Hall in London.

It was my graduation day!

It was filled with all excitement and also sealed with so much emotions.

I was wearing a black toga, neck lined with an orange silk. I felt really warm as I had a blue shirt and tie underneath. 'Twas a day of saying goodbye to all those boring lectures and sleepless nights doing all the homework and going into workshops and critiquing films, books and plays. Such a palava!

The Royal Albert Hall was magical and it seemed to be a momentous day for all of us graduates. It was packed as everyone's family came and some other spectators. My mama and papa came over, of course from France and I was so proud to share with them that very special day with my most distinguished award.

I hardly saw them when I was up on stage but was sure that they took a video and photos of me. What a great reward for after all those years spent in college. I was so glad that it was all over!

The ceremony didn't last too long although there were several speeches and intermissions but my family all ended up at the Ritz for an afternoon tea. I wasn't surprised when Kevin and Sandra came and joined us. They were present too, all throughout the ceremony. I was just a bit tearful, seeing all my loved ones on that special occasion.

Another surprise came when Claudio bumped at me whilst we're outside the hall waiting for the cab. He did not graduate unfortunately on that day but he looked well after being in hospital for a bit.

"Congratulations, Lean!"

He hugged and kissed me on my cheek. I was so glad he was there but also quite disappointed that he didn't make it to the stage.

"Summa cum-laude! How fantastic is that, mister!"

"I know! Can't complain, can I?"

We were holding each other's hands and I wanted to say many things to and tell and how I missed him. I wanted to see him too on stage and graduating with me. I cried but just once and hopefully that was it.

"I am sorry that you didn't make it."

"I'm sure next graduation day then, Claudio?"

"I hope so sweetheart!"

"We are going for an afternoon tea! Come, my family' here."

"Oh no, I have to rush home and pack as I am flying tomorrow for the States! "Thank you though!"

"Well, goodluck and best wishes, Clauds!"

"Lean! Come on, son!" Papa exclaimed as he was jumping on the cab with my mama.

"I'm coming, papa!"

"Bye Claudio!"

"Bye sweetheart, I'll keep in touch!"

He handed me a small bag and it looked like a special present but I just grabbed it and ran into the cab.

"Cheers! Thank you so much!"

I rushed into the cab and I saw mama and papa settled in their seats. They were staring at me with a lovely smile.

"That was Claudio. He is a really nice schoolmate but didn't graduate this time."

"A bit sad but there will be more graduations to come, won't it?"

They both nodded and the cab just left swiftly. I didn't even looked back and looked at him again.

I opened my present from Claudio and he wrote me a nice letter in a lovely card. He also gave me a gold painted diary from Harrods. He knew that I write a lot especially along my journeys.

We had a lovely afternoon tea and munches at the Ritz in Green Park. Kevin and Susan joined us too but just for a short period. Kevin gave me a red envelope and I was really excited to read their lovely card. A cheque fell down on the table when I opened it. My name was written on it with an amount of twenty thousand pounds from Devonshire Publishing. Fantastic!

"It's mainly a royalty for your coming book, Lean!"

"Thank you so much, Kevin!"

"This is amazing!"

The couple didn't stay long as Susan does all the time, as usual!

Mama and papa stayed at the Ritz for the night and invited me but I went out partying in Soho with my college friends that graduation night. My parents fled back to Nice the following day and I can't wait to see them again and visit the south of France. They left me in London with so much blessings. They trusted and respected whatever my decisions are in building up my career and my plan for the future.

Now that I have become more of an oyster on my own shell, I could see little things coming and beginning to life anew!

This is it! A new chapter and not the end or a closed book perhaps.

What is there to look forward for? Anything interesting to watch out for?

Let's wait and see...patiently.

"Inshallah...Alhamdullilah!"

www.ingramcontent.com/pod-product-compliance
Ingram Content Group UK Ltd.
Pitfield, Milton Keynes, MK11 3LW, UK
UKHW041943190726
13854UKWH00004B/1768